Camilla Isley is an engineer turned writer after she quit her job to follow her husband on an adventure abroad.

She's a cat lover, coffee addict, and shoe hoarder. Besides writing, she loves reading—duh!—cooking, watching bad TV, and going to the movies—popcorn, please. She's a bit of a foodie, nothing too serious.

A keen traveler, Camilla knows mosquitoes play a role in the ecosystem, and she doesn't want to starve all those frog princes out there, but she could really live without them.

You can find out more about her here: **www.camillaisley.com** and by following her on Instagram or Facebook.

@camillaisley
facebook.com/camillaisley

D1218030

By the Same Author

CAMILLA ISLEY

A Christmas Caroline

Christmas Romantic Comedy Book 2

This is a work of fiction. Names, characters, businesses, places, events and incidents either are products of the author's imagination or are used fictitiously. Any resemblance to actual events or locales or persons, living or dead, is entirely coincidental.

Dedication

To all the Scrooges and Grinches of the world, may you change your minds about Christmas…

And to moms: we rock!

And to dads who change diapers, and give baths, and read good night stories, you rock, too!

One

The Population Surplus

I refresh my inbox one last time, hoping to conjure a bold-font, all-caps subject line marked URGENT!!! that will give me an excuse to spend the night at the office.

But no magic salvation message materializes—only a bunch of last-minute holiday shopping offers. I click the email boxes in anger, wanting to snap the mouse in half.

Delete.

Delete.

Delete.

All the Christmas-loving idiots must've stopped working hours ago. They should all be boiled in their own pudding and buried with a stake of holly through their hearts.

The clock on my desk strikes three, leaving me no escape. Almost time to go.

From my corner office in the Wilkins and Marley tower, I stare out the windows at the mist clouding the city. Bleak, biting weather aligned with my mood. The dingy cloud engulfing New York City is so dense it obscures everything: lights, buildings, and Central Park—of which I usually have an unobstructed view. But the thick fog doesn't cover the angry sounds of the car horns blaring around Columbus Circle.

The scarce visibility must be causing all kinds of traffic jams around Manhattan.

I could use it as an excuse to stay longer and then blame traffic if I turn out to be late. But if I do, I'd probably end up stuck in the commuting madness and fully miss my family's annual Christmas carnage.

If nothing else, I should leave early.

Gosh, I hate the holidays.

With a heavy sigh, I accept my fate. I shut my laptop, a little too forcefully perhaps, and head for the coat hanger behind the door.

"Is *she* ever going to leave?" Debra's voice drifts in through the open door. My junior assistant is whispering, but not softly enough for me not to hear, especially not now I'm standing so close.

"Yeah, believe it or not, *she* has a family," Annabelle, the senior assistant, replies.

"What?" Debra hisses. "She's married?"

"No, nooo," Annabelle says as if the mere idea were absurd. "I didn't mean a husband."

"Right. Does she even *date?*"

"She had a serious boyfriend like ages ago when we were still working at Bucknam, but nothing ever since—that I know of."

"Really, who *was* the guy?"

"Sam Crawley, some kind of artist," Annabelle says.

A wistful pang squeezes my heart. I can't pretend that hearing Sam's name tossed around so casually leaves me indifferent, not even after all these years.

"Was he hot?"

"Very."

I have to silently agree. Looks were never a weak spot for Sam.

"And what happened?"

"I've no idea. One day he was on her speed dial, and the next, she instructed me to erase him from all her contacts."

"Sounds torrid."

"I bet it was. Anyway, we should be off the hook soon. Every Christmas she goes to visit her sister..." Annabelle pauses before delivering the punch line. "In Jersey."

"Are you kidding me?" Debra is rightfully shocked. "Caroline Wilkins in Jersey? I thought that if she ever crossed the Manhattan border to go anywhere other than Paris or Milan the soles of her Prada would auto combust."

I've had enough. I step out of the office, making them startle.

"Good evening, ladies."

"Good evening, Miss Wilkins," they return the greeting, their cheeks flushing different shades of crimson. The junior assistant blushes so brightly she matches my red leather boots.

"*She,*" I say pointedly, "is leaving and would like her car called."

"Of course, Miss Wilkins, right away." Debra scrambles to grasp the receiver and pushes the garage extension with trembling fingers.

One might say it's cruel to keep staff members so obviously terrified of their boss, but I'd respond that a little fear can go a long way in terms of efficiency.

"The car will be waiting for you downstairs, Miss Wilkins," Debra confirms quietly.

I nod curtly, imagining how she must be sweating under her cream polyester cardigan.

"Very well," I say. "Enjoy your holiday. And be here early on Monday," I say, happy that Christmas comes on a Saturday this year and they won't get any extra vacation days.

"Merry Christmas to you too, Miss Wilkins," Debra, the

most inexperienced of the two, dares to say.

Annabelle knows how much I loathe hearing the MC words; she lowers her eyes to her pleather boots, fully aware it was her responsibility to teach Debra to *never* wish me a merry Christmas. The mere sentence is an oxymoron.

I wince without responding and proceed to the elevator. Debra and Annabelle scramble to grab their things and follow me down the hall. When the elevator doors ding open, I step in and push the lobby button, enjoying the last glimpse of my terrorized assistants—they'll wait for *the next* one.

Just before the doors close, I lock eyes with Debra, and, wiggling the point of my left boot, I say, "These are Jimmy Choos, by the way."

After a split-second view of her jaw dropping, the doors seal me in, and the elevator begins its fifty-floor descent to the main lobby.

Nelson, my driver, is waiting for me in front of the building next to the company's black SUV. He's stamping his feet on the curb to keep warm, his breath pluming in the cold air. The moment he spots me pushing through the glass doors, he snaps to attention and opens the car door.

Now *that* is a well-behaved employee.

On my way to the car, two portly men in twin Santa costumes step into my path, blocking me. They're holding an assortment of brochures and flyers in their leather-gloved hands.

"Good evening, ma'am," the one on the right greets me, his fake white beard bobbing as he talks.

"Sorry, I'm in a hurry." I try to shake off whatever sales pitch they're about to palm off on me and sidestep them. But the two Santas mirror my movements and keep blocking the way.

"It'll only take a minute, ma'am," Left Santa says. "We're promoting literacy among less fortunate children, do you have kids?"

"No, I'm trying to decrease the surplus in population," I say ironically. I've seen enough friends and colleagues devolve their uteruses to those energy-sucking demons to know best.

"Well, you must have a nephew or a niece," Right Santa encourages.

Of those I have plenty, my sister shoots one out every couple of years—she's become more reliable than the tax man.

"I do," I say. "In fact, you're making me late for my visit to them."

"Then why don't you bring them the gift of a book?" Left Santa shoves in my face a bundle of pages that looks more like a pamphlet than a proper novel.

"Thank you, but I already bought them gifts." Correction, my assistants did and had them delivered to my sister's house.

"Then buy one for the poor. Christmas is such a hard time for those less fortunate."

"Pals, with all due respect, can you read the names on that building?" I ask, pointing at the skyscraper behind my back. Above the entrance, Wilkins and Marley is prominent among the names of other firms. "Mine's the big name on the left. I run a publishing house and I promise you I have all the books I need. Plus, we already sponsor"—I glance dubiously at the pamphlet—"legitimate programs to grow the next generation of avid readers. So, thank you, but, no thanks. Good afternoon, gentlemen!"

My tone doesn't leave room for a reply and the Santas

part to let me pass.

"Good evening, Miss Wilkins," my driver greets me, holding the dark SUV door open for me. "Were they bothering you?"

"Nothing I couldn't handle myself, Nelson. Thank you."

He nods and closes the door after I've gotten in.

As we head down Eighth Avenue, the fog and darkness thicken around us. Even without traffic, Nelson would be forced to proceed at a walking pace. At least I won't get to my sister's house too early; I can't stand to linger for more than a few hours and try to visit as sparingly as I can without creating a family feud. But Christmas Eve, like Thanksgiving, is mandatory.

Fan, my sister, bought a house two doors down from our parents'. I'd break out in hives at the mere consideration of sharing a zip code with our mother. A shudder runs down my spine as I try to absorb the warmth from the air vent. Actually, I'm not sure if it's the cold that's making me shiver or the idea of living in Jersey. But Fan swears that since she's had kids, being neighbors to Mom makes everything much easier on her. I can't imagine how.

I picture my top-floor apartment in the Upper West Side. I wouldn't swap the glass walls, clean surfaces, and huge closets for anything in the world. Not to mention I would never trade Manhattan with the suburbs. Not a chance in hell.

As Nelson and I make our slow progress through the city, the shop windows' lights glitter through the fog. Holly sprigs and decorations crackle in the heat behind the thick glasses and a swarm of people crowd the streets. Unreasonably cheery, last-minute shoppers who stroll around happy to throw their money at useless gadgets they'll give and receive tomorrow and then forget all about before the year is over.

My phone rings as we leave New York behind to enter Lincoln Tunnel.

"Hello?" I answer.

"Caroline," Yashika, one of my senior editors, says out of breath. "Glad I could reach you. I stopped by the office, but you were already gone."

The declaration bugs me for two reasons. First, because where was she an hour ago when I was desperately searching for an excuse not to leave? And second, because I don't like the idea, even implied, that someone could pull longer hours than me. I'm always the first in and the last out.

"Well, this is the one night of the year when I can't escape my family. I've tried, believe me," I say. "But what couldn't wait until Monday? We had nothing urgent on our plates if I'm not mistaken?"

"Actually, we did."

Yashika's seniority is the only thing that allows her to contradict me.

"Really?" I watch the concrete walls blur past as we make our way through the tunnel, a flurry of cars getting out of the city before Christmas. "What?"

"The option for *The Yellow Window* expires tonight."

"Yes, I'm aware. I've decided to pass."

The silence stretches between us before Yashika cuts through. "You've passed on *The Yellow Window?* Why?"

"I made Kendall Hick an offer, and her agent turned it down."

"How much did you offer?"

"Ten thousand dollars."

"But that's not nearly enough. That story is worth at least a six-figure advance."

"For a debut author with no existing platform? You

7

must've lost your mind, Yashika. I've already doubled what we offer to newbies. If Hick's agent thinks she can get more somewhere else, they're welcome to try their luck."

"But, Caroline, *The Yellow Window* is a masterpiece. I had to bust my ass to convince the agent to give us an exclusive option, and you're going to pass? Why? We have the money, haven't we?"

Irritated, I spat, "Maybe you should've also negotiated for the agent to have realistic financial expectations. And for your information, I had to spend a considerable chunk of our acquisition budget on securing our newest memoir. With the rest, I prefer to buy twenty new books for five thousand each rather than risking it all on a nobody."

Yashika's line goes quiet, and for a moment I can't tell if she hung up on me or if the poor reception in the tunnel cut her off.

Until her voice crackles back to life. "I can't believe you're throwing money at another ghostwritten celebrity bio instead of publishing the best book we've read in years."

"Celebrity novels sell. I'm merely making a business decision."

"It's the wrong one. Another publishing house is going to snatch *The Yellow Window* and make it a number one bestseller, and we're going to look like fools. You used not to care about profit that much. When I joined Wilkins and Marley, you were one of the best editors in the industry. You were ready to take a chance on new authors and you actually cared about the quality of the books we put out into the world."

"Well, that was before we had to compete with streaming services that let you binge unlimited content for less than ten dollars a month. And careful, Yashika, that's starting to sound awfully like a resignation speech."

"Of course it isn't," Yashika replies in a much more subdued voice. Guess her solid principles stop at the security of a paycheck at the end of the month.

"Well, if there isn't anything else?" I say, curt.

"No, Caroline, merr—I mean, have a good night."

I hang up without replying and stare out the window.

On the other side of the tunnel, we've officially crossed into suburbia. The bustling streets of Manhattan have been replaced by tidy rows of houses lining both sides of the road, Christmas lights hanging from gutters with plastic blow-mold Santas, and snowmen snickering from their perches on the lawns. Meticulously plowed driveways split the otherwise immaculate blanket of snow down the sidewalks. In the thick fog, the houses beyond are mere phantoms, indistinct and unrecognizable. But I don't need to see them to recognize every gate, postbox, and tree as we drive across my hometown. Until Nelson pulls up in front of yet another phantom house where the same plastic candy canes Fan has

Two

Leaks and Slips

"Would you like me to wait for you, Miss Wilkins?" my driver asks.

I meet his eyes in the rearview mirror.

"You'd rather go home, I expect?"

Nelson's gaze lowers with guilt. "If it isn't too inconvenient; it is Christmas Eve."

"It's not convenient for sure, but I suppose you must have the night like everybody else. Leave me the keys and call a cab. You can expense it."

"Thank you, Miss, but it's no matter. I'll walk a few blocks to the station and take the train back. In this weather, it'll be faster."

Nelson exits the car to open my door and once I'm out, he hands me the keys. One last goodbye nod, and he gets on his way to the station.

All too soon, I'm alone walking up my sister's driveway and slipping on the ice despite the pointy spikes of my leather stiletto heels—these should work as crampons.

I stop at the front door, allowing myself one last quiet minute. A Christmas tune is busting from inside the house, pouring out at every chink and keyhole, scraping against my skin. An ominous prelude to the chaos awaiting me within these walls.

I raise my hand to ring the bell, but before I can push the button my eyes fall on my sister's door knocker, which isn't at all particular, except for its largeness. Except now, I stare aghast as the tarnished brass surface transforms into Sam's face.

I haven't spared my ex-boyfriend of seven years a thought until Annabelle mentioned him earlier this afternoon. Was that enough to make me hallucinate him?

I try to blink the image away, but when I reopen my eyes his features, pale and wistful, are still there, aglow in a dismal light. Sam's expression isn't angry, but his gaze on me is the same as the day we broke up: disappointed, hurt, sad. His hair is curiously stirred, as if by a breath of hot air, and, although his eyes are wide open, they're perfectly motionless—fixed on me in that accusatory, regretful frown.

As my heart throbs under the relentless scowl, Sam's face disappears and the metal molds into a knocker again.

Startled, I squeeze my eyes shut and open them again to make sure he's really gone.

Yep. It must've been a trick of the light or something. I blame the hallucination on the lack of caffeine—I skipped my regular four o'clock double espresso today—and push my sister's doorbell.

Harper, Fan's oldest kid at age eight, comes to open the door, yelling, "Auntie Caroline." She tackles me into an embrace and drags me into the house.

An explosion of warmth and colors along with the smell of my mother's cooking replace the dingy fog and frost of the front porch.

"Mom," Harper shouts. "Auntie Caroline has arrived, I told you she'd be on time."

Ah, so the will-Caroline-deign-us-with-her-presence merry-go-round has taken place also this year.

I don't hear what Fan says in response if she replies; immediately after Harper's announcement, Fan's middle kids, Nora, five, and Benjamin, three, burst out of the living room and wrap themselves around my legs too.

They "help" me get rid of my coat, scarf, and gloves like little trained elves.

Nora also steals my bag and saunters back into the living room with the Prada tote slung over her shoulder and reaching to her calves.

The noise in this room with the tall ceilings and crooked wood floors is perfectly tumultuous. Instead of four kids, there might be forty for the uproar they're making. No one seems to mind. On the contrary, Mom and Fan are by the fireplace, laughing heartily, enjoying the raucous.

When Thomas, Fan's youngest at eight months, crawls to the couch and successfully steals Benjamin's toy car, his older brother manhandles—or should I say *kid*handles—him, prompting Fan to break them apart. On all fours, she gets in between her youngest to separate them and, at once, becomes the new attack focus. All the kids gang up on her. Benjamin pulls at her braid, tearing it half undone. Nora jumps on her back and tries to ride her like a horse, while little Tommy is quietly working behind the scenes to pluck off one of her shoes.

The scene is pure chaos, everything I don't want in my life and that makes me cringe watching. And yet... my sister looks so happy. A string I haven't stroked in years pulls in my heart, and I can't help but wonder if that could've been me if I'd stayed with Sam and we'd had kids. Another thought strikes me, who would our kids have taken after? Me? Him? Would they have laughed like Sam? His whole-heartedly laugh was one of the things I loved most about him.

But then I take another look at Fan's living room, at the mounds of discarded sticky toys and crayon stains adorning most surfaces, and at the stash of diapers she probably hasn't had time to put away, and I retract. No, thank you.

Harper comes standing next to me, arms crossed over her chest. "They're so juvenile sometimes, Auntie Caroline," she says, observing her brothers and sister with contempt. "Can I offer you anything to drink?"

"Thank you, Harper, I'm good for now."

My niece grabs a tray from a nearby coffee table. "A cookie then?"

I try not to wince at the tinge of artificial dyes on the sugar cookies. Gross. "No, thanks, I wouldn't want to spoil my appetite before dinner."

The festive atmosphere is already churning my stomach enough. Gag.

I'm scoping out where a safe place to sit would be when someone knocks on the door. In a rush, Fan shakes off Nora, scoops up Tommy, and, with her hair flying in all directions and minus a shoe, she rushes to the entrance.

"Hey, Caroline." My sister stops briefly by my side to greet me. "Sit down, get comfortable."

Then she carries on, followed by all her kids, to embrace her husband. Elijah comes stumbling into the house laden with Christmas presents.

At once my defenseless brother-in-law becomes the next victim of the shouting and struggling in an onslaught of miniature bodies.

Benjamin scales him, using a stool for a ladder. Nora picks his pockets. And even Harper, while not trying to get ahold of the presents, jumps on him from behind and, arms around his neck, rides him into the living room.

Elijah scrolls off his kids as a dog would with water, provoking even more shouts of wonder and delight. All the pillaged presents are recollected and placed in their rightful spot under the giant tree in the corner to be opened after dinner. At last, with all the adults finally present, we sit at the table.

The meal isn't any less anarchic than my welcoming into the house. Fan insists on maintaining "baby-led" weaning for all her kids. This means the children don't eat dinner before the adults or at a different table, but sit with us and have license to feed themselves however they see fit. In a nutshell, I can't protest when Tommy puts his dirty, chubby fingers on my plate to steal a bite of turkey or to squish my mashed potatoes and lick the puree off his knuckles. I don't know what sadistic instinct inspired my sister to place me next to the baby.

After a couple of hours around her kids, my temples are throbbing into a splitting headache. So much so that when the time comes to open the presents, I'm as eager as my nieces and nephews. Once this final consumerist ritual—great for book sales, I'm not complaining—will be completed, I'll be free to go. I brush off a stray smudge of gravy from my hand, a leftover from the baby slamming their fists down into their plate, and give the little monsters my presents to speed up the process. Annabelle always marks the packages with remarkable stickers so I know what I supposedly bought for each.

The unwrapping proceeds smoothly, the only bit of drama occurring when Tommy steals a doll's frying pan from Nora's new toy kitchen set, and the baby becomes more than suspected to have swallowed a plastic turkey glued on a wooden plate. And with all his imparted lessons on self-weaning, how to blame him?

My sister breaks into hysterics, expecting Tommy to go

blue and suffocate any minute. And when the turkey reappears at the bottom of Benjamin's slipper, she's ecstatic with relief.

Once the drama is over, the kids become gradually more subdued. Instead of running around screaming and playing with their new toys, they lie on the couch or in someone's arms, rubbing sleep from their eyes. One by one, they're brought upstairs and put to bed. Fan and Elijah work together as a well-oiled team. Benjamin goes first, then Nora. The youngest, Tommy, will go last as he still takes many naps during the day and is not yet time for his final feeding. When the time comes to put Harper to bed, Fan drops the baby in my lap in another shrewd maneuver.

The move surprises me so much, I don't have the promptness to complain. I remain stranded on the couch, with this miniature person in my arms.

We study each other.

Tommy looks up at me with big blue baby eyes and flashes me a one-toothed smile, followed by a happy gurgle. Kind of cute.

The baby reaches up for my hand and grabs one of my fingers with his tiny ones. A strange wave of heat flushes my cheeks and empties my stomach. A powerful emotion I can't describe, but that makes me deeply uncomfortable.

"Mom," I say when she reappears after tidying the kitchen for Fan. "You want to take little Tommy?"

"Caroline, he's just a baby." She sits on one of the twin armchairs by the fireplace next to my dad, who's reading the paper. "Holding him ten minutes won't kill you."

"I know, Mom, but I need to get going. The drive back to the city will take forever."

"You can't possibly mean to go in this awful weather,"

she protests.

"Why wouldn't I?"

"It's not safe to drive," Dad interjects, not looking up from his newspaper.

"It's as safe as when I came a few hours ago."

"That was different," Dad continues. "Nelson was driving."

"I have a license, you know."

Dad scoffs and eyes me over his newspaper. "You haven't been driving in, how long?"

"Dad, you're being melodramatic, it's just a little fog."

"A little fog?" My dad drops the paper on his lap. "Your mother and I had trouble finding our way across the street."

"And what's the alternative?" I huff. "I'm not spending the night on Fan's couch."

"Of course not, darling," my mom says. "You can stay in your old bedroom. We'd only have to make the bed."

I haven't slept in that room for exactly six years and three hundred and sixty-four days, and I'm not going to break the streak now.

"I'll call a cab then."

Dad arches an eyebrow over his black-rimmed glasses. "And how is putting your life in the hands of a perfect stranger any better?"

"I don't know, let's assume that if he or she is competent enough to get here safely, they can drive me back without harm."

"It would be safer to stay here tonight," Mom says.

I drop the argument with my parents, once they become so headstrong it's impossible to make them change their minds, and covertly order a car from an app on my phone.

Half an hour later, just as I get a notification that my

driver is five minutes away, Fan and Elijah come back down the stairs.

Perfect. I'm craving a good night's sleep in my California King bed. Mmm, I can almost feel the caress of my Egyptian cotton sheets. All I need to do is give Tommy back, say good night to everyone, and get the hell out of here.

I'm about to execute that plan when a sudden gush of wet warmth heats my lap.

I shoot up, holding Tommy away from me and yelping, "Oh my gosh, oh my gosh, he pooped on me." The move, unfortunately, brings his leaking bottom closer to my nose… Oh. My. Gosh. How can such a tiny creature produce such a potent stench?

"Shhh," Fan shushes me. "You'll wake up the other kids."

"Fan," I hiss between gritted teeth. "I'm covered in shit."

"It's just a little baby poo-poo." She takes her son back, cooing at him. "You've made your poo-poo, what a good boy." Fan doesn't even wince at the putrid smell. Either her nose isn't working, or becoming a mother for the fourth time has fried her few remaining neurons and they can't process signals anymore.

I rush into the bathroom and try to wash the literal crap out of my knit Fendi dress, but it's useless: the dress is ruined. I pull it off, careful not to make the contaminated patch come in contact with any skin or my hair, and trash it. Under the strong spotlights, I examine my tights, checking that no fecal matter has permeated through. Thankfully, it seems not. I still yank off my wool tights and grab a towel to scrub my legs thoroughly.

Now I'm clean, but I can't exit the bathroom in my bra and panties.

My phone pings with another notification.

Your driver is waiting for you at the address you provided.

Okay. I briefly consider stealing a bathrobe and walking out in that when my sister mercifully comes to check on me.

Fan knocks on the door. "Caroline, are you alright in there?"

"Yes, but I need clean clothes. Can you lend me something?"

Through the closed door, I hear Fan rustle in the adjoining laundry hall.

"Are sweats okay? I wear little else these days."

"Sweats are great," I say, cringing at the idea of borrowing the shabby mommy uniform.

I open the door and she stops on the threshold, handing me the clothes.

"What about your dress," my sister asks. "Did the stain come off?"

"No, it's ruined."

"Oh, maybe at the dry-cleaner, they can—"

"It's no big deal, Fan, I threw it away." Even if the stain *did* come off, I'd know it was there once. I'd never wear the poop dress again.

Fan's eyes fly to the bathroom trash bin and widen. "Gosh, Caroline, what is that, a two-thousand-dollar dress?"

Closer to three thousand, but I don't correct her.

Fan pouts. "Wow, it must be nice to have so much money you can literally throw it in the garbage."

I prefer to avoid the whole you-sold-your-soul-to-a-golden-idol dispute, so I purse my lips and pull on the black leggings and bright red Cornell sweatshirt Fan has given me. The fact amazes me every day that despite her Ivy League education, my sister chose to be a stay-at-home mom.

I zip up my boots and take a quick glance in the mirror. All I can say is that the Jimmy Choos could rock any outfit, even the suburban mommy uniform.

My ringtone goes off with an incoming call from the car company.

"Yes," I pick up. "Yeah, I'll be out in a minute," I reassure the driver.

"You're leaving?" Fan asks. "In this weather?"

Moving next door to my parents is slowly turning her into a carbon copy of my mother.

"Yes, in this weather, and before you can say anything, I'm not sleeping at Mom's." I hug her to prevent any further protest. "Thank you for dinner, everything was amazing," I tell Fan even if I know Mom cooked and not her.

I kiss my sister's cheeks and rush past her into the living room.

I collect my belongings from where my nieces and nephews have scattered them, saying my goodbyes and throwing around reassurances. Yes, the drivers from the car company are carefully vetted. And, yes, I'll text them when I get home to let them know I've gotten in safe.

I stuff my gloves, hat, and scarf into my bag—I won't catch a cold for a one-minute walk down the driveway and pull on my coat.

"Remember to text us," Mom pleads. "You always forget."

"Sure, Mom, I will."

Elijah walks me to the door and holds it open for me. "Good night, Caroline. Merry Christmas."

"Yeah, you, too."

I give him a quick hug and hurry down the driveway just

as my phone starts ringing again. Gosh, this driver must be an impatient prick.

I rush on the wet concrete, doing my best to keep my balance, but halfway down, the snow slush suddenly turns into a solid slab of ice, and the leather soles of my boots slip on the ice block as if greased, sending me flying.

I land with a hard tug on the frozen concrete, hitting my bum and head with brutal force as everything goes black.

Three

Christmases Past

I become conscious again to the sound of a monitor beeping, a persistent throbbing in my head, and a girl I don't recognize sitting at the foot of my bed—a hospital bed.

What the hell?

I stare to my right ·where a black monitor shows an electrocardiogram pulsating regularly. Cables jut from behind the screen and I follow one to a medical clip clasped to my index finger. On the other side of the bed, an empty IV stand is dangling above my head.

The room is tiny; it feels more like a cubicle. Between the bed and the left wall, there's merely enough space to host a leather armchair, for visitors I suppose, which is now empty.

I refocus on the girl sitting on my feet.

"Who are you?" I ask.

"Oh." She looks up at me through a curtain of white-blond hair so bright it's almost luminescent. "You're awake," she says, her voice soft and gentle. "And just on time." The girl lifts a finger as if waiting for something and, promptly, the chime of a bell resounds in the distance. Big and clear, like that of a church. "Right on the first stroke of midnight."

"Who are you?" I repeat. "Why am I in the hospital?"

"The answer to the second question is pretty straightforward: you bashed your head on the concrete after you ran out of your sister's house scared by a little diaper leak and landed yourself in a coma."

"I'm not in a coma, I'm talking to you."

"Technically, your *spirit* is talking to me. Your body is still out cold." She pats my feet over the blanket. "Don't worry, you're not dead, but you haven't gone back to the living yet, either. You're in a middle plane." She layers her hands one above the other. "Which brings us to the first question you asked. I'm Melodie, your assigned spirit guide."

I take a better look at her. The girl must be seven or eight, she's wearing a pristine white tunic trimmed with summer flowers and bound at the waist by a lustrous belt. In her hands, she's holding a branch of holly. But my eyes keep being drawn to the belt, which sparkles and glitters. The light parts, becoming dark and vice versa so that the girl's entire figure appears to fluctuate.

"Have you escaped from the pediatric wing?"

Or more the *psych ward.*

Melodie sighs. "A skeptic, I should've guessed from your file. You don't believe I'm a Christmas Spirit."

"Well, of course not."

"What about now?" she asks as her head disappears.

I yelp.

"And now?" Her head reappears, but floats in mid-air over no body.

"All right, all right, stop that." I touch the back of my head and find a huge bump just above my nape. The impact with my sister's driveway must've been a TKO.

The girl reassembles in one piece, head, body, and belt, and eyes me suspiciously. "You still don't believe me."

"If I say no, you'll make your head disappear again?"

"You know what, let's agree to disagree for now. Are you ready to go?"

"Go where?"

"Caroline, I thought you were this big-shot career woman"—she snaps her fingers three times in quick succession—"keep up! It's Christmas Eve, well, was Christmas Eve until a few minutes ago. Merry Christmas." Crazy Melodie makes jazz hands. "And I'm your spirit guide. Now, I know you Scrooge types are used to the five-star treatment: get a ghost to warm you up, then three separate spirits each on a different night, the whole shebang. Sorry, it no longer works that way. With the Christmas Spirit at an all-time low, we had to streamline our resources. So now you get only one spirit, yours truly, and we try to cover everything in one night."

"Cover what exactly?"

"Your *Christmases:* past, present, future. Come on, Caroline." She snaps her fingers again. "You didn't hit your head *that* hard."

"Listen, I still don't understand what business you have being in my room."

"Your welfare."

"I can assure you a night of uninterrupted sleep would be more beneficial."

"Your salvation, then."

"I don't need to be saved."

"Caroline, stop resisting me. You have a unique opportunity to take a hard look at your life and fix your mistakes—"

"What mistakes? I don't have any mistakes to fix. I have a wonderful life, a successful company I built from the ground up, I'm perfectly happy, thank you very much."

The spirit crosses her arms over her chest and eyes me like a professor would an unruly student, making me feel like the child between the pair of us. "What about regrets? Do you have any of those?"

Sam. The name pops into my head before I can do anything to prevent it.

"Just as I thought," Melodie replies smugly.

"I didn't say anything."

She taps her temple. "When you're with me, thinking is enough. Now, we should technically wait until one o'clock." The girl stares at the clock mounted on the sidewall of the hospital chamber. "But what do you say we get a head-start and get going?" She jumps off the bed and pulls off my blankets too quickly for me to clasp them.

Next, she grabs my hand and, with surprising force for a child, drags me toward the window.

"But it's freezing outside, and I'm wearing a hospital gown."

"Don't worry, you won't feel a thing."

"Can I at least put on some shoes?"

Melodie stops and eyes the far corner of the room, where a plastic bag with all my personal effects is resting on a chair.

"Haven't those boots done enough damage? Here, use these."

She hands me a sad pair of hospital slippers. While I put them on, she pushes the window open.

"Are you planning on flying?"

"Exciting, uh?"

"Not when you're mortal like me. I'd rather not splatter on the concrete, thank you."

"Don't worry; hold my hand and you'll be fine."

Melodie drags me along, and we pass through the hospital wall as if it were unsubstantial and walk right onto my parents' driveway. The city has entirely vanished. The darkness and the fog have vanished with it, and it's now a clear winter day, with fresh snow laid gently on the ground. We proceed along the driveway and once we reach the front door, we seep to the other side as if we were made of mist.

Inside, a thousand smells float in the air, each one connected with lost hopes, and memories, and joys long forgotten.

Fan, still only a girl, rushes down the stairs, screaming, "Mom, Dad? Where are you? Do I really have to wait until we get to Granny's house to open my presents?"

My sister runs clear past us, without sparing the ghost or me a second glance.

"They are but shadows of the things that have been," Melodie says. "They've no consciousness of us."

We follow Fan across the hall and into the living room, where nine or ten-year-old me is reading by the feeble fire.

"Caroline," Fan shouts. "You let the fire die down again."

Ten-year-old Caroline startles and looks up at Fan, then at the dying embers.

"Shoot!" She stands up and pokes the ashes with a fire poker while blowing air on the skeleton of the last log. Once the cinders turn a bright orange-red again, she asks Fan to pass her some kindling. The wood chipping burns quickly, producing enough flames for Kid Caroline to add another log in the fireplace.

"Phew," Kid Caroline blows the hair away from her face and messes Fan's bangs. "Good catch, Smalls, Dad would've skinned me alive."

"Why weren't you paying attention to the fire?"

"I was lost in my book," Kid Caroline replies, picking up Fan and sitting back on the armchair with her sister on her lap.

Fan grabs the hardcover from the armrest and turns a few pages. "This book seems really boring, Caroline, there aren't any pictures."

"That's because when you can read the words, you don't need illustrations anymore."

"Why not?"

"Because your mind"—Kid Caroline taps Fan's forehead—"can conjure all the images you want and a thousand more."

Fan doesn't look convinced and keeps turning the pages as if expecting a drawing to pop up, eventually.

"Where are Mom and Dad?" she asks when no magic drawings appear.

"They went to say hi to the Morales," Kid Caroline says, referring to our neighbors of the time.

"Do I have to wait until they get back to open my presents?"

"Yep."

Fan crosses her arms over her chest and pouts. Soon bored with sulking, she returns her attention to the novel. "What's the book about, anyway?"

"It's a story about sisters," Kid Caroline says, squeezing Fan closer.

"Two sisters?"

"No, four actually."

"And what's so interesting about them?"

"The story follows them as they grow into women, it talks about the men they love, the struggles they face…"

"What do you want to do when you become a woman?"

"I want to open a bookshop," Kid Caroline says with the certainty only a ten-year-old could have. "And fill it with the best books in the world and help all my customers find the perfect story for them."

My heart leaps in my chest and my eyes glisten at hearing my childhood dream spoken out so clearly. As an adult, I've accomplished much more than that. I've founded a publishing house, I do more than merely sell books. I produce them, select what gets out of the slush pile and into the world. And yet, the words of my younger self land on a heavy heart. My earlier phone call with Yashika rings in my ears louder than an alarm siren. When did the publishing industry become all about profit for me? When did I lose the passion for the actual stories I was publishing?

"What's the matter?" Melodie asks.

"Nothing," I say. "Nothing. I was just thinking about a phone call I had earlier, but it doesn't matter now. It's too late to do anything about it."

Melodie raises a white-blond eyebrow. "Is it?"

Meanwhile, in the living room, Fan claps her hands excitedly, asking, "And are the boys in the book cute?"

"Super cute." Kid Caroline grins and tickles Fan, who giggles along. "Laurie is the most handsome boy you'll ever find in a novel. You want me to read to you about him?"

Watching this, I sigh. I'd forgotten how close Fan and I were as kids.

"Yes, yes, yes, please do, Caroline, please."

"All right." Kid Caroline searches the book for the right passage and then reads aloud. "Jo liked the 'Laurence boy' better than ever, and took several good looks at him, so that she might describe him to the girls; for they had no brothers—"

"Just like us," Fan interrupts.

Kid Caroline taps Fan's nose. "Exactly like us, Smalls."

"Keep reading, keep reading."

"…They had no brothers, very few male cousins, and boys were almost unknown creatures to them. 'Curly black hair; brown skin; big, black eyes; handsome nose; fine teeth; small hands and feet, taller than I am, very polite, for a boy, and altogether jolly. Wonder how old he is?' It was on the tip of Jo's tongue to ask; but she checked herself in time, and, with unusual tact, tried to find out in a round-about way."

"Oh, Caroline, he does sound handsome. Will he and Jo get married?"

"I don't know."

"How could you not know?"

Kid Caroline laughs. "Because I haven't finished the book yet."

"Now I get why you forgot the fire."

"The fire," the sisters scream in unison and turn to the yet-again dwindling embers.

They scramble to revive them and when the flames crackle happily once again, Fan sits on her heels and with a solemn face asks, "Caroline, I know you already started the book, but would you read it for me? From the beginning?"

"Of course, Smalls."

Fan barrels into her sister, wrapping her arms around young Caroline's neck and covering her face with kisses. "You're the best sister in the entire world."

"Let's check out another Christmas," Melodie says, making me jump. I was so engrossed in the scene from my past, I'd forgotten a supposed spirit was beside me.

The room becomes darker, the wall panels shrink, the windows creak, and fragments of plaster fall out of the ceiling, showing the naked laths.

Uneasy, I say, "Let's go."

My parents' house disappears, replaced by the busy

streets of a city where gray, murky figures move back and forward and shadowy cars and cabs battle for the way in the usual strife and tumult that is New York City. The dressing of the shops in tinsel and frost makes it clear that, in this time, it is also Christmas. The evening is just coming over the city, the glow of streetlights starting to cast over the streets.

The ghost stops nearby a café and asks me if I recognize it.

"Recognize it?" I ask, baffled. "I camped in there most of my college years. Sam and I used to—" the words catch in my throat as a happy couple pushes out of the café, holding hands and laughing as the brass bell over the door jingles. A gust of brewed coffee and pine drifts out into the exhaust fumes behind them.

It's us.

College Caroline drags Sam down the sidewalk. "Come on," she says. "We're going to be so late. Mom is going to kill me."

"Kill *us,* you mean."

"Oh, please." She swats him playfully while still hurrying down the pavement. "As if Mom could ever find fault with you. Sometimes I think she loves you more than she does me."

"Well, that's because I'm extremely hard not to love," Sam says with a cheeky grin.

From the sidelines, I stare at his handsome face and it feels like I'm being hit in the chest by a wrecking ball. Gosh, I'd forgotten how ridiculously attractive Sam was. Unruly black hair, tan skin; big, black eyes—a real-life version of Laurie. Except no fictional character could ever match up with the reality of him. Sam is flesh and bones, warm laughter, and youthful enthusiasm.

Sam and College Caroline keep running down the street, holding hands and shouting, "Merry Christmas," to everyone they pass, breathless.

My eyes boggle. Was I really one of those insufferable persons who feel the need to overload cheers onto perfect strangers?

The ghost and I follow as College Caroline and Sam board a train to New Jersey.

I stop on the platform, undecided for a second. "Can we board a train?" I ask Melodie.

"Sure can." A cheeky grin comes over her face as she jumps on the car before me.

I hurry after her, and we find two empty seats facing Sam and College Caroline.

I gape incredulously as they start to make out, uncaring to be sitting in a very public space. We were one of those obnoxious couples who can't keep their hands off each other.

They pull apart only when the alarm on College Caroline's phone—a relic with no camera and no color screen—goes off.

College Caroline takes it out of her bag, silencing the noise. Sam tries to grab her again, but she deflects the attack, giggling. "Stop, I need to take the pill."

She blindly searches the bag for the tiny blister pack while Sam keeps distracting her by nibbling at her earlobe and kissing her neck. When she finally pulls the pack out, she's about to push a pill out when Sam covers her hands with his.

"What if you stopped taking it?"

"The pill you mean? Are you out of your mind?"

"Why? Would it be so bad?"

"What did they put in your coffee, are you high?"

I grimace at College Caroline's statement; I remember this conversation well.

Sam stares at her—me—unblinkingly.

The smile dies on College Caroline's lips. "You can't be serious! You want to have a baby, *now?*"

"Why not? We're young, we're in love, and I've always wanted to be a young father."

"But we're still kids ourselves, we haven't even graduated college yet. We should find out where we fit in the world on our own before we bring someone new along for the ride."

"No, you're right," Sam says. "I was just being impulsive."

Caressing his cheek, College Caroline says, "I love you, and I want to have your babies one day. Just not today."

Sam takes her hand and kisses the palm, "I love you, too."

She gives him a quick kiss and pops the little blue pill into her mouth. The train lights flicker and the ghost and I are once again side-by-side in the open air.

"Quick," Melodie urges. "Our time in the past grows short."

The scene changes and we land in my old bedroom at my parents' house. Sam and I are lying on my bed. The Caroline in this vision is still younger than I am now, but older and less carefree than the Caroline who was running to catch a train home with her boyfriend. There are new purple bags under her eyes, and her skin is a little ghastly. She looks exhausted, but still weirdly happy.

At once, I realize what day it is and subconsciously take a step back from the scene.

"Spirit, I don't want to be here. Please don't make me watch this."

"Sorry, Caroline, this is the one Christmas we can't skip."

Resigned, I return my gaze to the bed and the couple lying there. About-to-have-her-heart-broken Caroline is massaging her belly, complaining about having eaten too much and wanting to sleep.

Sam ignores the protest and kisses her neck. And she might've been over-full and tired, but not so spent as to resist Sam.

"Mr. Crawley, are you attempting at my virtue while under my parents' roof?"

With a devilish grin, he replies, "Miss Wilkins, I wouldn't dare."

A teasing smile comes over my lips. "Sure, you wouldn't."

She straddles him and tickles him. As a defense, he grabs her wrists and pulls her down in a kiss.

From the sidelines, I lose myself in that kiss once again, closing my eyes and trying to remember what it was like to kiss Sam, not knowing that would be our last kiss.

On the bedside table, Caroline's phone comes alive, vibrating inside her bag right on schedule.

My eyes fly open as my younger self straightens up to silence the alarm and take the pill. I remember that by the time I'd turned twenty-five, I did my best never to take the pill in front of Sam. I'd switched the alarm to a time of the day when I was usually at work and swapped the piercing ringtone for a more unobtrusive vibration-only notification. On the weekends, I stood on alert in the afternoon and sneaked off to the bathroom before the alarm even went off so that Sam wouldn't see me. Because every time he caught me taking the pill, his eyes turned sad, and I felt guilty. Either that, or we would outright fight about the right timing for us to have kids. Or even worse, he'd sulk in private and distance himself for hours. That small little pill had become the giant elephant in the room.

But that day, with all the excitement of Christmas, I'd forgotten all my precautions, and there we were on my bed, about to make love, with the nagging, insisting vibration of my phone as our soundtrack.

Caroline tries to climb off Sam and the bed, but he pulls her back, not letting go of her wrists.

"Don't take it."

"Sam," she says, already on the defensive. "I don't want a baby right now."

"When, then? It's been four years, Charlie Bear. You have a job now. We've been out in the world. I want a family."

"We're twenty-five, Sam. You make it sound like we're old crones or something, it's not like we're thirty." Being now two years past thirty, I scoff at how twenty-five-year-old me considered this to be old age. She, in the meantime, yanks her hands free and gets off Sam, sitting on the bed next to him. "And I don't want to just have a job, I want a career. It's easy for you to say when you don't have to give up everything."

"I can take paternity leave. We can put your career first if that's so important to you, I don't mind. It's not the Middle Ages. I can be a modern dad."

"Are you going to be pregnant and give birth, too? Breastfeed?"

I sound so harsh to my older ears.

Sam doesn't reply, but his jaw tenses.

"And you make it seem so easy, but I want to see how happy you'll be to deal with a screaming infant who keeps you up all night."

"That's why we should have kids now, while we're young."

"Sam, I'm not ready."

"You're not ready now, or you won't ever be ready?"

"I don't know, I can't speak for myself in five years—"

"Five years? Is that how long you plan to wait?"

"You know Jackie and I plan to leave Bucknam and found our own publishing house. It'll take at least that time to make it successful. We've worked on our five-year business plan nonstop for the last six months and there's no space in it for maternity leave."

Sam storms off the bed. "I don't want to wait that long."

"And I don't want to be forced into such an important decision when I've already told you I'm not ready."

Present and past me watch Sam's face turn from angry to sad, defeated, and then resolute. Both our hearts break. Hers for the first time, mine for the second as I wait to hear Sam's next words.

"Then maybe we shouldn't be together if we don't want the same things."

"Wow, Sam, if you want to leave so bad, no one's forcing you to stay."

I can't believe that's all I said. I watch impotently as my younger self lets Sam storm out of her room. Too proud to fight for him. I want to scream at her to do something, say something. Instead, I turn to Melody. "Spirit, I want to go. I don't want to see this. I can't bear it."

Melodie doesn't object as I push past her out of the room, running down the stairs of my parents' house.

Four

Christmas Present

As I jump off the last step of the stairs at my parents' house, my feet land on the white sterile tile of my hospital room instead of the living room carpet.

I'm back where this nightmare began, except, even in the present, there are two of me. I'm standing next to the bed while my counterpart is lying, eyes closed, hooked to various tubes and monitors. I don't even look like myself.

In a burst of light, Melodie appears beside me, panting. "Way to make an exit, Wilkins, it's hard to keep up with you."

"What's the meaning of this?" I ask, pointing at the me lying on the bed.

"Seems pretty obvious to me..." Melodie says, then taking in my baffled face, she adds, "Or not. This, Caroline, is your visit into the present Christmas."

"Why? I already know what's going on in my life. I don't need a refresher."

Melodie grabs her chin sardonically. "And don't you think that landing in a coma while trying to escape New Jersey deserves a moment of reflection?"

"No."

"Are you not interested in seeing how this affected your family?"

"If you're about to accuse me of ruining Christmas by slipping on the ice and hitting my head by accident, then, no."

Melodie raises her hand in a surrendering gesture. "All right, I'm not touching that, got it."

"How long do we have to stay?" I ask. Even in the spiritual dimension, hospitals still give me the creeps.

Before Melodie can answer, the door opens and my mom walks in. A nurse follows her, carrying a blanket and a pillow.

"I'm sorry we don't have any spare beds," the nurse says, dropping the blanket and pillow on the blue leather armchair flanking the bed. "But you wouldn't believe the number of domestic accidents we see at the holidays. People falling off roofs, drunken mishaps, kitchen disasters. But these chairs are the next best thing." The nurse fumbles with a lever in the back. "If you get tired, pull this down and the backrest reclines."

"Thank you," my mom says. "And merry Christmas."

"Merry Christmas," the nurse replies. "If you need anything, just push the big red button above the bed. I'll come back at three a.m. for a routine check."

The nurse exits the room, leaving my mom and Comatose Caroline alone in the silence.

Mom tests the chair mechanism and once she's grasped the operating principle, she sets the pillow and thin hospital blanket on the armchair as if she was making a bed. Before sitting down, she comes by the bed and caresses my hair.

"Caroline, my Caroline, you were such a happy child. And now you're..." She never ends the phrase, just bends over to kiss my forehead.

Then she drags the armchair a little closer to the bed and switches on the overhead light. After taking a book out of her handbag, she settles in.

The cover is so worn the title is no longer readable, but

even if I hadn't seen the novel in its original state just a few minutes ago, I'd still recognize it among a million.

"The doctors say it'll be good for you to hear voices, and this was your favorite story as a child..." Mom opens the book on the first page and begins reading aloud, "'Christmas won't be Christmas without any presents,' grumbled Jo, lying on the rug. 'It's so dreadful to be poor!' sighed Meg, looking down at her old dress."

"Spirit," I ask over my mother's voice. "Does she plan to spend the entire night reading to me?"

"I imagine so."

"But why?" The possibility of my fall being more severe than a freak accident crosses my mind for the first time. "What did the doctors tell her? I mean, I'm going to be okay, aren't I?"

"Yes, Caroline, you're more headstrong even than that ice you smacked your head on. Your prognosis is good. You have a serious concussion and they've preferred to keep you sedated overnight to give your brain time to recover without excessive stimulus. But other than a splitting headache you shouldn't suffer any long-term consequences—"

"The coma is medically induced?"

"Yes."

"Then why didn't you say so from the beginning?"

Melodie shrugs. "I have a flair for the dramatic."

I stare at my mom while she keeps reading in a low, calm tone.

"But if I'm going to be okay, why doesn't she go home? She has back problems and no matter what that nurse said, the chair can't be that comfortable."

"Ah," Melodie sighs cryptically. "Nothing is more powerful than the love of a mother for her child, but you

37

wouldn't understand that, of course. Do you want to go or should we stay awhile?"

"I want to listen a little longer, can I?"

Without waiting for Melodie's reply, I sit on the chair armrest, reading *Little Women* over my mom's shoulder along with her.

***

Mom falls asleep about halfway through the book. Her hands drop in her lap while she's still holding the novel, and her head lolls to the side. The blanket slides lower over her chest, uncovering her shoulders. I reach for it to tuck her in, but my insubstantial hands have no effect on the blanket.

The air on my other side brightens as Melodie and her weird luminescent hair come standing next to me.

"We have to go now, Caroline."

I nod and, even if I know she won't feel it, I kiss my mom on the temple before getting up.

"Where to now?" I ask.

"Ah, this is the bleakest part, I'm afraid. On to the future."

Five

Christmases Yet to Come

Once again, Melodie takes my hand and guides me toward the open window. Before jumping out, she stops briefly and throws me a side glance.

"A word of advice, as sad and dismal as our destination might be, keep in mind that you can change everything we're about to see." Then she jokingly punches her cheek. "Gosh, I'm such a wonderful spirit, you've been so lucky I got assigned to you."

I look down at her. "Really?"

"Oh, yes, you wouldn't have wanted a ghost of future Christmases as your permanent spirit guide. They're such a scary bunch. No matter how many times P.R. has told them to lose the black cloaks and liven up a little, they insist on traditions, creeping on their charges like mist. Plus, they explain nothing. Always pointing with their spectral hands. No wonder they get the worst results."

"What's P.R.?" I ask.

"Phantasm Resources, same as HR for humans. Anyway, this winter all ghosts of future Christmases have been suspended since their performance last year came in so abysmal. And while I'm stuck working with you, they're in London attending a social skills seminar." Melodie shrugs. "Or maybe that was their evil plan all along to skip work."

"Y-you have ghost retreats in *London?*"

"Yeah, the buggers are staying at The Langham Hotel— very spirit-friendly institution, let me tell you—getting the

39

five-star treatment, while the rest of us suckers are stuck working all night."

My head spins with the notions of phantasm resources and spirit seminars overseas. Let's hope this is just a bad dream and that my medically sedated brain is only playing tricks on me.

Instead of concentrating on the absurdity of everything Melodie just said, I humor her and call her out on her bullshit.

"That doesn't seem like such a poor deal since you work *only* at Christmas."

"Eeeeh." Melodie grimaces. "That depends."

Depends on what? I want to ask. I hope she isn't planning to haunt me even once this dreadful festivity is over.

But she doesn't leave me time to voice my doubts as she squeezes my hand and drags me out the window. Just before we step into the void, she turns to me and says, "And, Caroline?"

"Yes?"

"Not a dream."

From the high window of my hospital room, we land in a suburban neighborhood of orderly townhomes dressed up for the holiday season. If I had to guess where we are, I'd say not New Jersey. In my spirit form, I can't feel whether the temperature is warm or cold, but no snow covers the front yards, and no icicles dangle from the tree branches—which incidentally are mostly palms, and the grass is green and lush. Not a wintery look. We could be in California or Florida or Nevada—one of the southern states.

Melodie guides me to a pretty house painted in a deep burgundy with white lining. Inside, a couple in their mid-fifties is having lunch.

"Are you sure you don't want to go to the funeral?" the husband asks.

The woman stabs the chicken breast on her plate with aggressive slashes. "Jerry, I've already told you, I don't want to take a six-hour flight to be in New York for just a day."

Ah, California, then.

"It wouldn't have to be a one-day trip, we could make a holiday of it. You always tell me you miss Christmas in the snow, and New York is fabulous this time of the year."

The wife takes a bite of the chicken and finishes chewing before replying, "That would be in even poorer taste than not going to the funeral. If you want to see New York at Christmas, we can go next year, darling." She reaches for his hand across the table and squeezes it. "When it'll be just a vacation."

"I'd love that, honey. But are you really sure? She was your aunt after all."

The woman lets go of his hand with the excuse to grab a loaf of bread, which she proceeds to tear to pieces. "So? She didn't come to Mom's funeral, did she? And she always refused to visit us for Christmas. She never called. Not for a birthday, or when our kids were born, or when *their* kids were born."

"She sent cards."

"*Her secretaries* sent cards. I'm telling you, Jerry, she came to our wedding only because Mom was still alive and she was too ashamed not to show up." The wife shreds the bread loaf in even smaller pieces, eating none. "I'm not wasting a trip to New York for that woman. I've arranged with the funeral house to cremate her, and she already has a spot at the cemetery in the family plot next to Mom and Dad. They'll bury her the day after tomorrow, and if no one shows up to her wake, that's her doing not mine."

The husband's eyes widen. "Your brothers and sister aren't going either?"

"Not that I know of. They're younger and knew her even less than I did."

"What about the—" the husband coughs and his neck and ears turn red. "...err the inheritance. Did she leave a will?"

"Her lawyer hasn't contacted me, and even if she'd left it all to us, I'm not sure I'd want that woman's money." The wife dries a tear from her eyes. "She tore Mom's heart away little by little and didn't even bother to visit her sister before she died. I don't want to talk about her anymore. I don't want to spare that witch a thought ever again."

The husband pauses. "Sorry, I didn't mean to upset you. I won't bring her up again."

"Thank you." Eyes still glistening, the woman goes back to cutting chicken that definitely doesn't need more slicing.

Once the conversation between husband and wife is over, the house dissolves, and Melodie and I jump right into the heart of New York City, or better, the city seems to spring on us, encompassing us of its own will.

We arrive at the corner of Fifth and 57th, amongst the shops and the usual New York varied crowds: tourists, students, nouveau riche, old wealth, models, professionals, and artists.

Melodie stops near a knot of businesswomen, evidently meaning for me to listen in to their conversation.

"No," a woman in a black power suit and stylish black coat says, "I know little about it either way. I only know she's dead."

"When did she die?" another one asks.

"Last night, I think."

"Why, what was the matter with her? Was she sick?" a third says, taking a sip out of a bottle of Kombucha tea. "I thought she'd bury us all."

"Who knows," the first woman replies, peeking at her

watch.

"What has she done with all her money?" a red-lipped woman asks. Judging from the level of swelling of her lips, she must've come fresh out of a filler appointment.

"I haven't heard," the woman in the black suit says, checking her watch again. "She hasn't left it to *me* for sure. That's all I know."

The joke is in poor taste, but is received with a general laugh.

"No, seriously, I don't even know if she had any surviving relatives." The woman now lowers her voice. "It's likely to be a very cheap funeral," she adds. "I think her attorney is organizing it, and for the life of me, I don't know anybody who'd want to go. Should we form a delegation and volunteer?"

"Will there be favors?" a young woman in a stylish fur jacket asks.

"It's a funeral, Freya," the first woman replies. "Not a wedding. Anyway, I'll go if anyone wants to come with me. I'll shoot you a group message with the time and place, all right? But now I have to go." She air-kisses her audience goodbye, and both speakers and listeners stroll away.

I don't know any of those women, so I raise my eyebrows at Melodie searching for enlightenment. She just points at a two-person meeting happening a few paces away. I listen in again, thinking the explanation might lie there.

I don't know these women either. But their fashionable-while-professional clothes mark them once again as part of the business crowd. Magazine executives, art gallery directors; they could be anything.

"How are you?" one says.

"In a hurry, like always," the other replies in a thick British accent. "Heard the news?"

"About the old hag?"

"She finally got her own, hey?"

"So I'm told," the first woman says, shuddering. "Cold, isn't it?"

"Seasonable for Christmastime. You're not a skater, I suppose?"

"No, no. I leave that to the tourists. Well, it was good seeing you."

"And you."

Not another word. That's their meeting, their conversation, and their parting.

I'm again surprised Melodie should attach importance to conversations apparently so trivial; she must have some hidden purpose.

Are they supposed to lead me to my future self? I can't deny I'm curious to see myself in my golden age. Have I aged well? Or should I book a Botox appointment the moment I wake up from the coma?

I search the surrounding faces for my image but can't find myself anywhere. We leave the busy avenues of the Upper East Side and move into an obscure part of town, a dangerous neighborhood, a place respectable people shouldn't wander into. The streets turn to alleys, foul and narrow; the shops and houses become wretched; and the people ugly. Drug dealers on every corner, drunkards stumbling off the curb, and prostitutes soliciting clients. The roads are dirty and like so many cesspools, they disgorge their offenses of smell and dirt and life upon the straggling concrete. The whole neighborhood reeks with crime and filth and misery. Far in this infamous den of thieves and lost souls, sits a low-browed, beetling pawn shop, below a penthouse roof, where jewelry, watches, trinkets, and heirlooms are sold.

An old man appears behind the rusty glass door. He takes

a suspicious glare at both sides of the road and swings the open sign to closed. He then locks the deadbolt and with one last wary look at the empty street, retreats inside.

Melodie gestures at me to follow him. And despite the locked door, we seep through the glass and rusty iron right into the obscure shop.

The man is not alone, we find. A woman with a heavy bag slung over her shoulder is looking at him, as if waiting for instructions. She keeps shifting her weight from one foot to the other while turning her gaze gingerly from side to side. And if there ever was a prize for a shady pair, these two would win it.

"Come into the parlor," the man says. "It's better if we discuss this deal in the back."

He pulls aside a frowzy curtain of miscellaneous tatters, revealing a space behind. The old man turns on the lights with a flick of his finger. Then, he grabs an ancient stair-rod and rakes the dying fire. Once a small flame burns from the ashes, he drops the rod and leans against the antique desk placed at the back of the room. He opens a leather box and pulls out a cigar, lighting it with a match, never taking his eyes off the woman.

As he sucks in the first dregs of smoke, the woman throws her duffle bag on the threadbare rug covering almost the entire room, and sits on a stool in a flaunting manner, crossing her elbows on her knees and looking at the old man with bold defiance.

"Mrs. Dilber, please," the old man says. "The suspense is killing me, what's the loot?"

With the top of her shoe, the mysterious Mrs. Dilber pushes the still-closed bag toward the man. "See for yourself, old Joe, and let me know the value of it. Speak out plainly."

Keeping the cigar nestled between his thin lips, old Joe

kneels on the carpet. With greedy fingers, he unzips the bag and lays the treasures within in an orderly line onto the rug. He takes out one designer bag after the other. Prada, Fendi, Gucci, Balenciaga, Louis Vuitton, Hermes…

Old Joe stands up again, drops his half-smoked cigar in an ashtray, and begins inputting sums into an old calculator.

When he's reached the total, he turns the calculator toward Mrs. Dilbert, saying, "I always give too much to ladies. It's a weakness of mine, and that's the way I ruin myself."

The woman gives a stiff nod, as if she disagreed on the over-generosity of the offer, prompting old Joe to round the desk and count bills out of a drawer.

Mrs. Dilber approaches him, eager to get her paws on the sum, but old Joe snatches the wad away and casts a sidelong glance at the woman.

"Any chance someone will come looking for them bags?"

Mrs. Dilber shakes her head. "They belonged to a dead woman with no close family; she won't need them where she's gone. They'd have been wasted if it hadn't been for me."

"What a good soul you are, Mrs. Dilber."

"What can I say, it's not my fault if the old crone scared everyone away while she was alive, and I won't be ashamed to profit when she's dead! Ha, ha, ha."

I listen to this dialog in horror and watch with equal detestation as the shadows of the fire dance on their evil grins transforming the two crooks into obscene demons who might've been marketing the corpse itself.

"Melodie!" I say. "Can we leave this place now? I might become sick."

I recoil in terror as the scene changes once again, and I wind up almost touching a bed on which, beneath a ragged sheet, lays a corpse.

The room is very dark, too dark for me to distinguish any details. But a pale ray of light falls straight on the bed, allowing me to see the plundered and bereft, unwatched, unwept, uncared for, body of a woman. A secret impulse makes me anxious to discover whose room it is, whose body.

I glance at Melodie, her gaze fixated on the woman's head. The cover was so carelessly adjusted that the slightest rising of it, the motion of a finger on my part, would disclose the face. I think about it, feel how easy it would be to do, and long to do it; but I have no more power to withdraw the veil than to dismiss the specter at my side.

A cat tears at the door, restless and disturbed. And before the scene turns into the urban legend of the crazy cat lady who died alone and had her cat eat half her face before she was found, I step away and walk straight on frozen grass.

Melodie and I reach an iron gate, and I look around before entering. We're in a cemetery, walled in by houses; overrun by weeds, the growth of vegetation's death not life; choked up with too much burying.

Melodie moves expertly among the graves, leading me to one. Ah, are we to learn the identity of the dead woman?

I creep toward her final resting place and read upon the headstone of the neglected grave, a solitary name with no epigraph. Caroline Wilkins.

Six

Christmases That Could've Been

The graveyard shrinks, collapses, and dwindles down, transforming into the hospital chamber.

I turn to Melodie and clap my hands. "Bravo! Extra point for that last dramatic flair."

The spirit pouts. "That didn't scare you?"

"No, I'm not afraid of dying. Death is the only certainty we have in life. Well, that and taxes," I say, pretending not even the scene at Harper's house shocked me. Because that woman we saw living in California and stubbornly refusing to attend her aunt's funeral must've been my oldest niece.

"But aren't you afraid to die *alone?*"

"We all die alone. And what you showed me isn't my future," I reply, dismissing the possibility that I wouldn't visit Fan on her deathbed. "But one of the million futures that could await me." If I were to turn into a heartless asshole.

"Well, Caroline, I'm sorry to say, but that *will* be your future if you continue on your current path."

"So, what do you expect me to do? Wake up from the coma, give all my money to the poor, and what? Board the merry Christmas wagon? Join a carol choir, perhaps? Please."

"Actually, Caroline, no. I never expected a single night of introspection to make you see the light. I warned them upstairs"—she points at the ceiling—"you were going to be difficult. But I enjoy a challenge,"—she cracks her knuckles enthusiastically—"and, anyway, I'm more of a show don't tell kind of gal." Melodie elbows my upper thigh. "Like my literary puns?"

"How long have you been waiting to drop that line?"

She smiles. "Pretty much all night."

I give her a thumbs-up. "You have a future in stand-up comedy. But, as much as I've enjoyed your company, my dear ghost, you're just a figment of my imagination and I can't wait to wake up from this coma to be rid of you forever."

"Not so fast. I *have* to make you see my point first."

"And how do you propose to do that?"

"Anticipating how stubborn you'd be, I devised a little independent study for you."

I clap my hands in mock excitement. "Oh my gosh, please tell me I'm going to join the five-star ghost retreat in London."

"Not quite. See, tonight, we've visited Christmases past, present, and future, but in my many years on the job, I've determined that the most powerful Christmases to show to a lost soul are the Christmases that could've been. That's why I'm sending you on a little field trip."

I roll my eyes. "Another one? We've been bouncing around all night. I thought my brain needed to rest. How am I supposed to recover if you keep dragging me all over?"

"Don't worry, this time you'll be flying solo. I mean, I'll still be nearby, but I won't be as hands-on as I've been so far."

"You'll be gone? For real? Tell me where do I have to sign?"

Melodie chuckles. "No contracts, we're not infernal spirits after all. Christmas ghosts work completely free of charge, you can keep your soul. Just take my hand and we can be on our way."

Without giving me time to agree or disagree, Melodie grabs my hand, and in a whirlwind of light, I start falling and falling until I land on a soft bed, feeling so drowsy I struggle to keep my lids open.

"Where am I?" I ask.

"At home," Melodie whispers in my ear, while her annoyingly shiny hair is the only thing that prevents me from falling asleep on the spot. "And keep in mind, you've just hit your head pretty hard. If you can't remember stuff, claim short-term amnesia and you'll be fine. Goodbye, Caroline, sweet dreams..."

The light dims, and I sink into the pillows and close my eyes.

***

A high-pitched wail pierces through my sleepy brain. I pull up on my elbows and blink at the surrounding room. I'm not in a hospital chamber, but this isn't my apartment either. The furniture in this place is run-of-the-mill cheapish and covered in scattered clothes. My housekeeper would never let my house get to this state of disarray. And the clothes themselves are nothing I'd be caught dead in. Half of them because they're *male* clothes, and the others because they scream suburban housewife with no sense of style.

I touch the back of my head, and, yep, the bump is there, still tender.

"Merry Christmas, Charlie Bear." Sam—an older version to that of my nightmare of last night—appears on the threshold, and I blink harder.

He's as tall and handsome as ever. But his dark hair is longer than when we broke up, and as he smiles at me, his eyes crinkle with more lines. But other than that, he's my Sam. I stare at the inch of bare skin between his white T-shirt and gray sweatpants and my body goes into overload: my mouth waters, my heart swells, and my belly contracts... not to mention the lower regions, which seem to have suddenly become wide awake and alert.

"Look who's already up on Christmas morning," Sam says, cradling a bundle in his arms. "Someone must be hungry."

He deposits the bundle in my arms—a bundle that turns out to be a brown-eyed baby with a wisp of black hair—and kisses me on the forehead.

Like a total creeper, I inhale his scent, closing my eyes and savoring the familiar fragrance of cardamom, sage, mixed with the dry crispness of vetiver. Armani Acqua di Gió, still, always, his perfume.

In the two seconds I've been busy smelling my ex, the baby in my arms has gotten down to business: he's pushed my unbuttoned night blouse aside with his little hand and has closed his bare gums on my right nipple. I yelp in surprise as he begins suckling on my boob.

I stare up at Sam in a panic, not sure what to say.

He talks first. "I'll just hop in the shower really quick while you feed him, you can go next."

Sam disappears behind another door, and I'm too shocked to reply. I stare back down at the baby attached to my breast. My first instinct is to pull him away, but he's not having it. He's latched on for dear life.

I expect the nursing to hurt, but it doesn't. I don't feel much at all, actually. Until, after about a minute of sucking, my nipples contract, and fluid gets pumped out. In fact, the boob that's not currently being sucked by the baby spurts milk like a fountain.

I search for something to stifle the flooding and find a stray towel on the nightstand. I push it onto my left breast until the stream stops.

After a while, the baby lets go of my left nipple but doesn't appear content. I stare down at him and at my bare chest. One breast is soft and somewhat saggy while the other is engorged and seems ready to burst. I swap the baby around and give him the hardened breast, he takes all of a half second to latch on and suckle away happily. The more he sucks, the more the bursting sensation fades, leaving me oddly satisfied.

I've just barely sighed in relief when I realize I shouldn't be at all relieved about successfully breastfeeding an infant, because a) I have no children, b) I'm not married to Sam—no matter the rose-gold wedding band on my ring finger, and c) I don't live here. Where the hell am I, anyway?

Before I can process all these impossibilities, the baby detaches and looks up at me. I stare into his brown eyes, an exact replica of Sam's, and when he smiles at me, my chest swells in response—not my breasts, but the beating part behind the rib cage. I'm waiting for a major epiphany to happen, one in which I realize my entire life has been a total waste… Instead, the baby lets out a sonorous burp and regurgitates half the milk on my chest, which promptly shrinks back to a reasonable, babies-are-awful size.

Sam comes out of the bathroom at that exact moment, wearing only a towel around his waist. Droplets of water glisten on marble-like skin and flat muscle. And, oh gosh, where did the six-pack come from? I might not be digging the baby thing, but give the baby daddy to mama.

How on earth is it fair that I'm seeing him for the first

time in seven years and he looks like that while I'm covered in baby vomit and spilled breast milk?

Sam sits on the bed next to me. "And how are my two munchies doing?"

"It threw up on me!"

Sam blinks at me. "*It?*"

"Yeah, the baby."

"Caroline, are you okay?"

"No, I'm a bit confused." In a flash of memory, I see Melodie's face hovering next to mine and whispering, *"...keep in mind, you've just hit your head pretty hard. If you can't remember stuff, claim short-term amnesia..."*

That little minx, she must've sent me into a parallel universe or something. "I hit my head, I have amnesia," I blurt out.

Sam's forehead creases with worry. "What's the last thing you remember?"

I'm not sure how to reply, since I don't know how my life unfolded in this timeline. But, judging from the baby in my arms and the ring on my finger, Sam and I must've gotten back together at one point and he must've prevailed on me about the kid thing. The only safe answer would be... "You were breaking up with me because I refused to go off the pill."

"But that was seven years ago!" Sam rubs a hand on his forehead, even more worried. "You don't remember falling in the driveway?"

"Well, yeah, the ice was slippery and my Jimmy Choos weren't exactly the best shoes, but—"

"Jimmy Choos? Charlie Bear, you don't own a single pair of Jimmy Choos."

I have a baby and no Jimmy Choos?

Please kill me now. In what circle of hell has Melodie sent me?

"Are my Prada gone, too?"

"Honey, you're delirious. I'm taking you to the emergency room like I should've done last night."

Not another hospital. Last time I went, a ghost haunted me and shipped me here.

I try to rationalize with Sam. "On Christmas Day? It's going to be total chaos. Sam, I'm fine, really."

He crosses his muscular arms over his still-wet chest. "Tell me the name of your son and you can stay put."

I look at the bundle in my arms, who has fallen asleep after his morning snack.

Baby names, uh? What would've I named a boy? Surely something after a character from one of my favorite books. Not Laurie, because I've always thought of Sam as my Laurie, and if I ever had a daughter, I would've wanted to call her Josephine. And I wouldn't have wanted two siblings named after two star-crossed lovers. The next obvious choice would've been Mr. Darcy. But I wouldn't have named a baby in the modern era *Fitz*william, which leaves only one possibility...

Chin up, I defy Sam's scrutiny, and say, "William."

He winces. "Almost, Caroline, that's our other son's name."

My eyes bulge. "We have more than one kid?"

"We have three. Jo, Will, and little Bram," he says, pointing at the sleeping baby.

Ah, Bram, yeah, that would've been my second-best choice for a boy's name, after Bram Stoker, the inventor of Vampire Lit and my personal hero.

"Sam, you're overreacting," I still try to say. "And we

can't possibly drag three kids to the hospital."

"No, we're leaving them with your mother."

"Please, it'll take her forever to come here from New Jersey."

Sam stands up abruptly. "That's it, Caroline, we're going *right now.*"

He turns around and drops the towel on a chair, regaling me with an unobstructed view of his round, totally biteable bum. I know I should avert my gaze, that I'm acting like a total creep, but, gosh, if the man isn't sweet of heart and fine of ass.

The show quickly ends as he pulls up a pair of boxer briefs and jeans and a sweatshirt over his head.

"But why?" I protest.

"Because we *are* in New Jersey."

"We don't live in Manhattan?"

"No, we live right across the street from—"

"Please don't say right across the street from my parents." I jolt upright, making the little bundle in my arms protest in his sleep.

I stand up and drop the baby into Sam's arms, my palms going clammy with cold sweat. I cross the room to the French windows and pull the curtains aside to reveal an unobstructed view of my parents' house across the street, and on the right, three houses down, is my sister's two-story.

"And Fan is next door?"

"Yep," Sam says, eyeing me with an increasingly alarmed expression.

"Oh, I'm *so* going to *kill* her," I hiss under my breath.

"Who? Your sister?"

"No, not Fan. Melodie."

"Who's Melodie?"

I wave him off. "It doesn't matter. You wouldn't understand."

I can tell he's confused but goes along with it. "Are you ready to go?"

"I can't go covered in baby puke."

"Then take a shower while I bring the kids over to your mom's. Charlie Bear, this is serious." He closes the distance between us and, securing the sleeping baby in a one-arm hold, cups my face with one hand. "I want to make sure you're alright."

Sam stares at me, his eyes brimming with worry.

"You don't find me repulsive," I say, matter-of-factly. "I'm frazzled, covered in baby puke and spilled breast milk, and you still like me."

Brown eyes all stormy and intense, Sam kisses me on the nose. "I do a little more than like you. I love you." He rests his forehead on mine while an explosion goes off in my chest.

POW!

I haven't heard him say these words to me in forever. I'm pretty sure in my universe the real Sam no longer feels that way about me. But here...

Sam withdraws. "But now, chop, chop, I want you showered and ready to go to the hospital when I come back."

***

"Caroline, what are you doing?"

Sam's voice makes me jump and I turn away from the closet, throwing another rag dangling from a hanger on the bed.

"I'm trying to find some of my clothes," I say, nonplussed. After a quick shower where I skipped washing my hair, I came back into the bedroom to get dressed, but couldn't find anything to wear.

Sam's eyes widen and his jaw tenses. "But *all* your clothes are literally on the bed."

"These hand-me-downs? I don't think so. Everything in this closet looks like it came from a consignment store."

"What's gotten into you, Caroline? There's nothing wrong with your clothes."

I scoff. "Yeah, right, go tell that to someone who doesn't have a sense of fashion."

Sam puts a hand on his hips. "Let's hear it, Miss Fashion Victim. Where do you usually shop?"

"Barneys, Bloomingdales, Saks Fifth Ave," I pull on the collar of another shapeless black dress to read the label. I've never heard of this brand before. "Definitely not wherever this thing came from."

"I swear you've never set foot into any of those luxury stores."

"And why wouldn't I?"

"For one, we can't afford it."

I gasp, letting the dress I was holding drop to the floor and covering my chest with my hands. "Oh my gosh, are we poor?"

"No, Caroline," Sam says exasperated. "We're not poor, but we bought a four-bedroom home in one of the most expensive towns in—"

"New Jersey." I wrinkle my nose.

"—in an amazing school district, and we have two other mortgages on your shop and on my studio."

"My shop?"

"Yeah."

"I own a *bookshop?*"

Even without my recent stroll into Christmases past, I would've remembered my childhood dream, but maybe I wouldn't have made the connection that quickly.

"Yes."

"You mean a single, physical location."

"Yep. I mean, after a few more payments."

"What about my publishing house?"

Sam's eyebrows furrow together. "What publishing house?"

"The one I founded after leaving Bucknam Publications and taking all their best authors with me?"

"Charlie Bear, I don't know about taking all their authors, but you left Bucknam after going on maternity leave for Jo and never looked back."

"But why would I have quit if not to start a company?"

Sam blinks. "You wanted to spend more time with Jo and needed more flexible hours, plus the commute to Manhattan was a bitch."

"So, I became one of those suburban moms who never go back to work?"

"You *went* back to work. You bought the shop."

"Aaargh." I put my hands in my hair. "What a cliché. I'm so going to kill Melodie."

"Who is this Melodie?"

"My Christmas ghost."

Sam presses his lips together and with no further comment rummages among the clothes spread on the bed and hands me a navy-blue potato sack.

"Put this one on, you always liked it."

I take the sack and eye it dubiously.

"And I don't care if it doesn't adhere to your new fashion sense, we have to go *now*."

"What's the hurry?"

"You've started talking about ghosts, that's the hurry."

"I knew you wouldn't understand if I told you about Melodie. And I don't care what you say, I'd like to look presentable before we go."

"We're going to the emergency room, not the Met gala."

"But what if I run into a cute doctor?"

Sam crosses his arms over his chest, narrowing his eyes. "What, indeed?"

I'm so used to being single that the words spurted out of my mouth before I could think.

"Sorry," I say. "I didn't mean it like that. I'll go get changed."

I carry the potato sack with me and go hide in the bathroom, away from Sam's disapproving gaze.

"Melodie," I hiss to the empty air, trying to summon my tormentor. "Your plan is not working, you know? If anything, it's proving *my* point. Can I go back to my life now?"

No one answers me.

"Melodie? You said you'd be around if I needed to—"

"Who are you talking to?" Sam's voice comes from the other side of the door.

"No one." I frown at the empty room one last time. "I'll be right out."

Seven

Motherhood 101

"Are you experiencing any blurred vision?" A young doctor—probably someone at the bottom of the pecking order who got stuck working on Christmas Day—asks me.

"No," I say, dangling my feet off the examination table.

"Please follow the light with your eyes." He waves a thin flashlight in my face, and I dutifully track it with my gaze.

A nurse knocks on the door and comes in to hand the doctor a file. He clicks the light off and looks at whatever the nurse gave him.

His eyebrows rise slightly. Is it an okay-good rise or an oh-my-gosh-she's-gonna-die rise?

I anxiously follow the upward and downward progress of the doctor's eyebrows as he keeps reading. After all, even in my real life, outside this crap parallel universe, I was in a medically induced coma. If the same fall happened in this world, why didn't my family bring me to the hospital last night? Shouldn't they have been more invested in my well-being?

The doctor clears his throat, interrupting my thoughts.

"Your scans came back, and they're negative for intracranial bleeding. The swelling in your brain is minimal and probably going down as we speak. How are you feeling?"

"Like someone who has been bashed in the back of the head with a baseball bat?"

"Ah, yeah, that's normal, the headache will persist for a

few more days, but I can prescribe you painkillers for that."

"She's breastfeeding," Sam interrupts.

The doctor winces. "In that case, I'm sorry, nothing stronger than Tylenol. Take a max of six pills per day, no more than two at a time and at least four to six hours apart."

"Isn't the maximum dosage *ten* pills per day?"

When I have long days at work, migraines are par for the course and I pop Tylenols like candies.

"Yes, but since you're breastfeeding, what goes into mommy"—he points at my chest—"goes into the baby, so a lower dosage is preferable."

Oh, great, moms don't even get the good drugs or enough of the crappy ones. They have to keep their headaches. Way to go, Melodie, your independent study is truly selling the "quit your job, be a mom" lifestyle.

"And what about her memory?" Sam asks.

Sorry, Pal, I want to tell him. My memory will never come back because this universe doesn't exist. You're never getting back your perfect Mommy Caroline.

"Your wife is suffering from traumatic amnesia, which means her memories should likely return as the injury heals. But there's no telling when—or, in the worst case, if ever. Some patients never recover."

Sam does his best to keep a straight face, but I can tell he's not happy to be saddled with this new grumpy model for his wife.

"Is there anything we can do to speed up the recovery?" he asks.

"The best course would be to stick to old routines." The doctor now turns to me. "Caroline, surround yourself with familiar faces, go back to work if you're not still on maternity leave—you will increase your chances of remembering things."

Aha, fat chance. "Thank you, doctor," I say nevertheless.

"Other than the memory loss and the bump," the doctor concludes, "you seem perfectly healthy and are cleared to go home and enjoy the day."

Aha, double fat chance. I've never hated Christmas more.

I'm not sure if the look on Sam's face is relieved or worried as he asks, "Should we be on the lookout for any other symptoms, doctor?"

"If she gets lightheaded, faints, falls for no apparent reason, or throws up, rush back to the emergency room immediately."

"Thank you, doctor," Sam says. "Merry Christmas."

Shiny and bright!

***

Sam pulls up in front of "our" house, kills the engine, and turns to me with a heavy sigh, evidently preparing to give me a pep talk.

"We should discuss how to handle the kids," he says.

"What do you mean?"

"Jo is old enough to understand what happened, we can tell her the truth. Bram is too small to notice anything is wrong but Will wouldn't handle the news well. He's already having trouble coping with the arrival of Bram and wouldn't be okay with the idea of his mommy not remembering him or…"

I cross my arms over my chest. "Come on, say it."

"Not loving him."

I'm not sure how to respond. Should I feel guilty for not loving a kid I've never even seen?

"Caroline, I get it."

"I don't think you do," I say.

"Well, not really. But I can try to put myself in your shoes. You wake up this morning thinking you're twenty-five and that we just broke up and, instead, you find out we're married, have three kids, and live in New Jersey. I get it, it's a lot to take in."

"It really is."

"Charlie Bear, I'm not asking for you to be back to normal, I'll help you out as much as I can, but if you see Will and don't have any kind of epiphany remembering who he is at once, please *pretend* you love him."

"I'm a proud bookshop owner, New Jersey wife, mother of three, and I love my kids," I say, nodding. "Gotcha."

We get out of the car and cross the street to my parents' house just in time for lunch. Before we can even knock, Harper runs out and wraps herself around my legs closely followed by Nora.

"Auntie Caroline, you're okay! We thought you might be dead."

"No, Harper, I'm fine." I touch the swelling on my head out of reflex. "Just a bump. Nora, go back in, you're not wearing a jacket, and it's cold outside," I say, acting more attentively than I would normally, the memory of the future scene at Harper's house still fresh in my mind.

Sam gapes at me.

"What?" I ask.

"You remember their names!"

"Well, of course, I do, they're my nieces."

Sam doesn't say the words out loud, but we both know what he's thinking: why can't you remember the names of your own *kids,* then?

"I'm not the brain whisperer, Sam," I say in a low voice

so only he can hear me. "I don't know why only certain memories are gone."

Well, I do know, and it's because they never happened. Our marriage, the three kids, it's all a fake. But I don't want to make another trip to the hospital or to be committed as a mental health patient, so I stick to the amnesia story.

With a bright, I-dare-you-to-complain smile, I add, "Shall we go in?"

I carry Nora in my arms while walking hand in hand with Harper.

Inside the house, I drop Nora on the hardwood floors just in time for Benjamin to barrel into me as I'm squatting on the floor to let his sister down.

"Benjamin." I ruffle his hair.

He stands on his toes and kisses my cheeks. "I'm greeting you, Auntie, as the Europeans do."

"How sophisticated of you, Benjamin."

Behind my nephew's shoulder, I spot a shy boy, two-and-a-half maybe three years old, leaning against the arched living room threshold. And no one needed to tell me he's mine and Sam's son. William has Sam's curly black hair and straight nose. And while his eyes are also the same brown as Sam's, the shape is all mine, as is the mouth.

"And who's that handsome young man over there?" I ask.

Sam is standing behind me, and, even though I can't see him, I sense he's following the exchange with his heart in his mouth, holding his breath.

Don't worry, hubby, I don't traumatize kids for fun.

Will rubs his eyes with the back of his hands as if he'd just woken up or, more likely, if he'd been about to cry.

"Mommy," he moans.

"It's okay," I say, while still squatting down on the floor.

"What's wrong?"

"Harper said you were dead."

His cousin gasps in outrage. "I did not say she was dead. I only said that I overheard Grandma say Auntie Caroline was at the hospital and that my friend's mother went to the hospital and never came back because she died there."

"Well, I'm most definitely not dead," I say. Then, opening my arms for Will, I add, "You want to give Mommy a hug?"

He rushes toward me and wraps his little arms tightly around my neck, burying his face in the nook between my neck and shoulders.

I hug him back and, while I don't experience any kind of epiphany, there is something powerful in the moment. In becoming someone's safe harbor. Will is hugging me like I'm the most important person in the whole wide world, the utmost center of his universe.

I straighten up with him wrapped around my body like a mini koala and carry him into my parents' living room, finally making it past the entrance hall.

My mom has a baby in her arms, but I can't honestly tell if it's Bram or Tommy, Fan's youngest. Since another baby is sleeping in a crib next to the couch.

That's the last panicked thought that crosses my mind before my family assails me with questions.

"How are you?"

"What did the doctors say?"

"Is your memory—"

"Not in front of the kids," Sam interrupts.

On the couch, another girl, younger than Harper but older than Nora, is doing her best to avoid my gaze. The girl has my eyes—color and shape—and my straight hair, while the rest is all Sam.

That must be Jo. She was smiling before Sam and I entered the room, showing a cute tooth gap, but now she's sulking quietly. Ah, we must have a complicated mother-daughter relationship.

I'll have to question Sam about it later.

I sit on the couch while still holding Will, who doesn't seem to have any intention of letting go, and greet my daughter, "Hey."

"Hi, Mom."

No, how are you? Good to see you're not dead. Apparently, a mutter "hi" is all I'm going to get.

Will finally stops hiding in my neck and some inexplicable primordial instinct takes over and prompts me to kiss him on his chubby cheeks, repeatedly, until he has to push me away, laughing and giggling. I feel possessed.

"Will," Sam says, squatting down next to the couch. "We have to talk to your sister in the other room. Could you let Mommy go for a few minutes?"

"Can I play with Lightning McQueen?"

"Sure you can."

"Okay."

Will smacks an absurdly loud and partly wet kiss on my cheek and hops off the couch while Jo sighs next to me and gets up, crossing her arms over her chest.

With a sullen pout, she asks, "Where do you want to go to talk?"

"Grandpa's studio," Sam says.

We all shuffle into my dad's home office, and Sam closes the door with a soft click behind us.

Jo immediately climbs on Dad's leather chair and spins around, reminding me terribly of myself at her age.

"Jo, would you stop spinning for a second," Sam says. "We need to have a serious talk."

Jo stops the chair to face us and, cross-legged and cross-armed, continues to sulk.

Once we have the resentful attention of our daughter, Sam, standing awkwardly on the other side of Dad's desk, explains the situation. "Sweetie, after you went to bed last night, Mom went to search for Mr. Whiskers-Winkle in the garden because he hadn't come home yet."

What kind of creature is a Mr. Whiskers-Winkle, I wonder, but don't ask aloud.

"But he was sleeping with me in my bed," Jo protests.

"We know that now, but Mom didn't, so she went outside and slipped on the ice, hitting her head."

Jo stares at me with an indecipherable expression, a mix between wariness and being sorry for me.

"Earlier, we had to go to the hospital because Mom fell harder than we initially thought, and the thing is, sweetie, Mom has amnesia."

"You mean like Anastasia after Rasputin tries to take her?"

I raise my eyebrows.

Sam turns to me and explains, "It's one of her favorite cartoons." Then, speaking again to Jo, he confirms, "Mom can't remember what happened last night..."

Jo gives me a hopeful side glance before asking, "How far back does the amnesia go?"

Sam pauses undecided, "About seven years. The last thing she can remember happened before you were born."

Jo doesn't look the least heartbroken at being forgotten by her mother. Instead, she looks up at me with a glint of relief in her eyes. I smell smoke, *lots* of smoke.

"But that doesn't mean Mom doesn't love you," Sam keeps consoling a child who evidently needs no cheering up. "She still loves you, but you have to be patient and help her as much as you can in the next few days until her memory comes back. And you also have to promise not to tell your brother, it's important."

"Okay, Daddy, I promise." She hops off the chair. "Can I go now?"

"Not so fast," I say, pinning her down with the signature mean-boss stare I use when I want to terrorize my employees.

"Sam, would you mind if I had a word with Jo alone?"

"Why?" My husband seems anxious at the prospect of leaving me alone with one of our kids.

"Oh, nothing, we need a mother-daughter chat, that's all."

Sam still seems unsure, but then looks around the studio and presumably assesses there are no mortal dangers, and that not even this alternative version of his wife could do many damages, because he nods. "I'll leave you ladies to talk, then."

As soon as the door clicks shut, I round the desk and lean against it on Jo's side.

"So," I say, giving her the evil eye once again. "Care to tell me what's really going on here?"

"Nothing, Mom," Jo says, gazing at the points of her shoes. "I'm really sorry you hit your head and got hurt."

"Nu-uh, that's not it, don't play games with me. Why are you happy I can't remember you?"

"As Daddy said, I know you still love me deep down," she says in an angelic voice I don't buy for a second.

I narrow my eyes. "If you tell me the real reason, there won't be repercussions, whatever it is. But if I find out on my own… I can't make any promises." Then, before she can deny it again, I tap the side of my temple. "Remember, no one knows when all those memories might come back." She doesn't need to know the answer is *never ever.*

Jo theatrically rolls her eyes. "We had a fight last night, okay? And I'm just relieved you can't remember it."

Ah, bingo.

"What was the argument about?"

"I asked you for a phone and you said I wasn't old enough."

Damn right.

"How old are you again?"

"I'll be seven next September and I'm in the first grade." She sits up taller. "I'm not too young."

"You're definitely too young. The only electronic device you can get at your age is an eReader."

My daughter's mouth gapes open. "That's exactly what you said last night."

"Well, I might've lost my memory, but I'm still me. And I guess you didn't take my refusal as a young lady mindful of her manners," I say, citing *Little Women.*

Jo's eyes drop to the floor once again. "No."

"And what did you say?"

"I called you a mean old bitch," she mumbles. I'm shocked for all of two seconds. I've been called worse. "And you replied that mean old bitches didn't buy presents for their bratty daughters and that I wouldn't get anything today." Jo puts her hands forward as if to prevent me from confirming the punishment. "But you said you wouldn't punish me if I told the truth, I can open my presents today, right?"

"I don't know," I say. "Would you like to add something else in your defense?"

Big blue eyes stare up at me. "Yes, Mom, I'm sorry I called you a mean old bitch."

I still haven't decided if I should be more offended at being called old or a bitch.

"Aaaand," I prompt impatiently.

"And I promise I'll never call you names again."

For someone with zero mothering experience, I'm nailing this.

"All right, apology accepted. Let's go join the others before Grandma's turkey goes cold or something."

The moment we walk back into the living room, my mother hands me a stinky baby.

"Ah, just in time to change his diaper."

I take the poop-bomb, holding Bram, presumably, at a safe distance from my body, and pass it along to Sam. "I don't change diapers."

He takes our son from me. "Excuse me?"

"I said I don't change diapers."

"Why not?"

"It's gross and I wouldn't know where to start."

"Well, since I'm going back to work on Monday, you'd better learn quickly. And you're in luck because I can give you the clean-*le-cul* crash course right now."

"Saying it in French won't make it any less gross," I say.

"*Mon chéri.*" Sam bats his lashes. "Please follow me *dans la salle de bain.*"

I trail my husband into the downstairs half bath which is equipped with all kinds of scary baby equipment: a changing table, wipes, diapers, and other obscure things I can't name or fathom a use for.

Keeping the baby in a one-arm hold, Sam begins his lesson. "First off, make sure there's a clean underpad on the changing bed."

"Why?" I ask. "Isn't the cotton cover enough?"

"In case of a leak, you don't want to have to wash the cover every time. Then you gently lay the baby on top and check the damage." Sam unbuttons the baby's romper and pulls it off his chubby legs, raising it high above his belly. He repeats the process with the body underneath until the diaper is finally revealed. Sam tears it open and, oh, gosh, the room turns into The Bog of Eternal Stench.

"Agwhk," I gag. "What is *that?*"

"Oh, don't be such a wuss. This is only milk poop, wait until he moves on to solids, those are the real stinkers."

"You mean worse than this? How's that even possible?"

"It is, believe me."

Sam grabs our son's ankles in one hand and lifts his bottom off the changing table to remove the diaper and to wipe his tiny butt.

"And we've had a leak," he says, assessing the brown stain on Bram's white body. Ew. The poop has raised up to at least half of the baby's back. "We're going to need to change him completely."

"Okay? Where are his clothes?"

"I left his bag in the hall."

"I'll go get it," I say, ready to do anything to get away from this smell.

"That's the other thing, Caroline." Sam stops me. "If something like this happens when you're alone with Bram, you can never ever leave him on the changing table."

"Why not?"

"Because he may roll over and fall."

"Okay, so what do I do if I need clean clothes?"

"The safest thing is to put him on the floor on a towel, not much harm he can do from there."

"Never leave the baby alone on the changing table, gotcha."

I run out of the room and breathe in a gulp of fresh, poop-free air. By the time I come back into the bathroom with Bram's bag, the smell isn't as awful. "You got rid of the Eau de Poop," I say. "How did you do that?"

Sam points at a white plastic bin in the corner. "Diaper Genie."

Bram chuckles. He's naked except for a clean diaper and his old clothes are sealed in a plastic bag.

"Should I put those in the Diaper Genie as well?" I ask.

"No, they're washable, you know." Sam chuckles. "If we had to throw away all the rompers he poops on…"

"You just put them in the washer full of poop?"

"No, you hand wash the poop first, and then throw them in the washing machine."

"Ew, poor Maria."

"Who's Maria?"

"My housemaid."

Sam blinks at me, and another dreadful realization hits me.

"We don't have a housemaid, do we?"

"Nope."

"And who does all the housework?"

"We do, and now Jo has taken on some basic responsibilities like bringing out the trash."

"But wouldn't it be easier to hire a housemaid?"

"We have help, the same lady who cleans the shop comes to the house twice a week to give us a hand with the bigger things, but now's the holidays and she's off to visit her family in DC." Sam looks like he wants to pinch his nose.

"And, as for the mortgages and college funds, twice a week is all we're comfortable paying for."

"Oh, okay," I say, thinking the last time I did any house chore must've been at least five years ago.

We both gloss over the topic, and Sam undoes and re-fastens Bram's diaper to show me how to do it. To the baby's delight, we work together to re-dress him and finally get out of the bathroom.

But the moment I move away, Bram howls like a wolf on a full moon.

"What's wrong with him?"

Sam bounces him. "He must be hungry."

Before I can reply, my nipples go rigid and become utterly uncomfortable.

Sam stares in horror at my general chest area. "Charlie Bear, did you put on your nursing pads?"

"What are nursing pads?"

"They prevent you from leaking milk onto your clothes." He points at my chest.

I look down where two twin dark stains are spreading in a circular halo around my nipples.

"What's happening?"

"You're leaking breast milk."

"Why?"

"It's a natural response to the baby crying, your body wants to soothe him."

We walk back into the living room where my sister takes a two-second look at me and mercifully comes to the rescue. She grabs a heavy blanket from the couch and takes Bram from Sam's arms, wrapping the baby in a warm cocoon.

"Let's get you home and changed," Fan says to me. "I'll explain everything about breastfeeding."

Joy to the world.

***

Half an hour later, I've changed into a breastfeeding wool dress with side breast pockets. Underneath, I'm wearing a detachable bra padded with nursing pads, and I'm holding Bram over my shoulder, waiting for him to burp as per my sister's instructions.

"Sometimes it helps if you hold them upright and bounce them gently on your legs," Fan says.

I follow her suggestion, holding Bram from under his armpits. The little mothersucker seems to enjoy this novelty and chuckles away content until a monster burp escapes his lips.

Fan rewards him with a shower of compliments, "What a good boy, what a beautiful little boy."

Bram basks in the praises until his face contorts into a grimace, goes all red and another, more sinister gurgle comes out of his other end just before the now-familiar stench of baby poop invades my nostrils.

"Oh," Fan cheers. "Someone has gone poopy-poop, good boy, good baby you."

"Again?" I say. "Is he sick? Should we call the doctor? He already pooped thirty minutes ago."

"Don't worry," Fan reassures me, as she offers to take the baby from me and change him. "He just fed, it's completely normal to go again. Babies can poop up to five times per day, sometimes more, when they're breastfeeding exclusively."

"Five times per day?"

My sister waves me off. "But you're almost past that phase. Once they're weaned, they only go once or twice a day, tops. Solid foods are much better."

Famous last words.

Back at my parents' house, Fan and I have to duck out of the way as an angry Will throws a projectile of mashed potatoes in a screaming fit.

"I don't like it. I'm not eating it."

Since we sat down at the table, my sister took all of ten minutes to feed Benjamin—who, also in this universe, is self-weaned and ate on his own—while the rest of us have alternated in a dance of pleads, threats, and games to convince Will to eat.

I turn toward my sister. "Didn't you say solid foods were better?"

"Unless you have a picky eater." Fan pats my leg. "Give it another year or two and you'll be out of the woods, I promise."

The idea of another year here is so tragic I almost laugh. I sure hope Melodie isn't planning to leave me in this suburban hell for more than a day because I don't care if she's a ghost and supposedly already dead, I'm going to find a way to kill her again.

Eight

Presents

On Christmas night, once all three kids are miraculously fed and asleep, I collapse on the bed ready to sink into a coma again. Gosh, being a mother is like having a full-time job. No, correction, it's like having *three* full-time jobs with a house to manage, a husband, and another actual job on the side.

My eyes are already half-closing when Sam comes into the room, holding a large present. A thirty-by-twenty-inch rectangular box wrapped in shiny gold paper and with a silver ribbon on top.

My husband smiles in a goofy way. "We usually exchange presents on Christmas morning, before the kids get up and the whole circus begins, but we never got a chance today."

When he drops the gift on the bed, I notice a smaller red box sitting on top of the larger one.

Thank goodness in this universe I'd already bought something for him.

I smile, because, heck, what girl doesn't enjoy opening a present from her loving husband? I know the situation is weird, with this Christmas ghost reality, but I can't help myself from enjoying being with Sam again, at least in these private moments.

"Which one is mine?" I ask.

Sam sits on my side of the bed. "Big one."

I pick up the smaller red box and hand it to him. "Gosh,

yours weighs a ton."

He takes his present and rattles the package. "Mmm, wonder what it is, you go first."

I pull on the silver ribbon and tear the gold paper underneath to reveal a plain white box. Inside, wrapped in white tissue paper, lies a silver evening gown. I scoop the dress up, and the fabric is like liquid in my hands—silk.

I stare at the label, and my eyes goggle. For all his talks about mortgages and college funds, he sure didn't pull punches in choosing my present.

I stand up and lay the evening gown against my body. The line is simple with spaghetti straps and no decorations, but the front and back are beautifully draped, and the long skirt reaches to my toes.

"Sam, this is beautiful. Thank you."

"You're beautiful. You shouldn't have let the dress go, it was made for you."

I walk up to the closet and stare at myself in the mirror.

"I did?" I ask, trying to remember the last time I saw something I liked and didn't buy it for myself. "Why?"

"Well. We can't really afford it, but it's Christmas…"

I turn and smile at Sam, feeling more emotional than I should, considering I've been able to afford the most expensive fashion for a while now. And while this dress might not be as pricey as some of the items in my real closet, it feels all the more precious.

"Is it for a special occasion?" I ask. The silk dress is definitely not everyday wear.

"Yes, New Year's party."

I can't help my curiosity. "Where?"

"New York City, baby."

I force myself to keep smiling. Has New York, my

beautiful city, become a fancy destination in this life?

"Go on," Sam says. "Try it on."

I consider for a second moving into the bathroom to change. In my head, Sam hasn't seen me naked in seven years, but in this reality, he probably knows my body better than I do. Still, I turn away shyly as I shimmy out of the black leggings and breastfeeding dress. Sam's eyes burn a hole in my back all the same, so to distract him from my semi-nakedness, I say, "Go on, open yours, I'm curious to see what it is."

I pull on the dress straps and admire the final result in the mirror. Wow, Sam is right, this dress *was* made for me. It fits like a glove and it holds onto my mommy curves in all the right places. My boobs look majestic in this universe. Must be all that breast milk.

I turn to thank Sam once again and find him staring down at my present with tears in his eyes. Oh, gosh, is Jersey Caroline so unskilled at gifting that she made a grown-ass man cry?

"Was my gift that awful?" I ask.

Sam looks up at me. "To the contrary."

He drops the box on the bed and stands up. His muscular arms wrap around me and he gives me one of those Hollywood kisses that don't belong in the real world. And good thing he's supporting me because my knees buckle under the heat of his mouth. I'd forgotten what it was like to be kissed by Sam, and this kiss might surpass all the ones I do remember. I'm his wife now, and we're a couple who must've shared many struggles and grown into a solid team battle after battle.

When Sam lets me go, I stare into his dark eyes. *Why did I ever give him up?*

The level of intensity is too much too soon. I pull away, blushing like a schoolgirl while trying not to freak out from the unusual intimacy.

"I must give superb gifts in the future, if this is the reaction I get," I joke, and go pick up my present for Sam.

The red wrapping paper is discarded to the side, and a plain black box about the size of a book sits on the comforter, a flat round stone inside it. A single word is etched on the stone's surface: yes.

I pick up the engraved stone. "And you could make sense of this?"

"Mm-hm."

"What is it?"

Sam takes the rock from me, smiling and shaking his head as he sits back on the bed. "It's a yes, written in stone."

I blink, still confused. "Care to explain?"

Sam caresses the stone with his thumb and looks up at me. "A while ago, I told you I wanted to try for another girl. And you were skeptical because, you know, another pregnancy, we'd have to clear the attic, start another college fund... You said you'd have to think about it; that it wasn't a definitive no, but that I shouldn't get too excited because it wasn't a yes written in stone, either." Then he shows me the rock. "Guess you made up your mind."

Another baby? They—I mean, Jersey Caroline and Sam—want another kid? Aren't three enough? Are they nuts? I've been a mother for less than a day and I'm already more exhausted than after a one-hundred-hour week.

Sam must read the terror in my eyes. "Don't worry, we don't have to try to get pregnant at least for another year. Doctor's orders are to wait for a minimum of eighteen months between pregnancies. And I know you've gone from being single and twenty-five to being in your thirties and married with three kids overnight, but I'm sure your memory will come back."

No, Sam, my memory won't come back because this place isn't real. I'm probably just dreaming about you while lying in a coma in a hospital bed in Manhattan.

Given the circumstances of this fake world, I don't see the harm in making Sam happy.

I go to him and bury my hands in his hair, lifting his head up to look at me. "I'm sure it will. Thank you for being so patient with me." I kiss him on the forehead. "Now, I'd better get changed before I ruin the dress."

I change quickly, replacing the dress on its hanger with extra care and hanging it outside the closet so as not to wrinkle it. Sam changes T-shirts and I steal the warm one, putting it on just like I used to do when we were together.

As I join him in bed, he eyes my PJ of choice and smiles. "Some things at least never change."

I scoot under the covers and kiss him on the cheek. Sam cups my face and kisses my mouth, then my jaw, my neck, and collarbone.

While my body comes alive under his touch, my mind is screaming at me to pull the brakes. I've had plenty of casual, meaningless sex in the past seven years with strangers I can't remember. But the last time I've made love was with Sam on Christmas Eve, all those nights ago. I'm not sure if I'm ready for the intensity of it.

But then Sam's hands sneak under the T-shirt, caressing my upper thighs, and all reason flies out the window. I'm about to rip the clothes off his back when Bram starts cry-screaming in the adjoining room.

"Oh, oh," Sam says, letting me go. "Someone's ready for

his midnight feeding."

I curse under my breath and get off Sam, pulling on a robe.

In the nursery, Bram is waiting for me, kicking his tiny legs and arms up in the air. I tap the cactus night-lamp to increase the level of luminescence and pick him up.

"Hello, little mothersucker, you know you just prevented Mommy and Daddy from having the best I-haven't-seen-you-in-seven-years sex?"

Bram gurgles, satisfied.

"Happy are you, uh?"

I sit us in the rolling armchair, open the top of my robe, pull up the T-shirt, unhook the bra flap, and offer him my nipple.

Bram latches on with the voracity of a piranha. The usual initial pinch comes, followed by the tingling response as the milk flows.

My son places his little hand on my breast and looks up as he suckles.

"Nu-uh, not working," I say. "I don't think you're cute."

I rock in the chair, and after a while, his eyes close.

As with Will before, I can't resist the impulse to bend down and smell his head while planting a kiss on the small whiff of hair that grows on top.

"Don't get any ideas in this little head of yours," I whisper. "I don't like babies."

I rock on and study his peaceful face now that he's asleep in my arms. The straight nose, long black lashes, plump, kissable cheeks, and perfect lips.

"I don't like you."

Nine

How's The Husband?

Breakfast the next morning is a mess. Burned eggs, spilled milk, an empty box of cereal, coffee brewing without water in the tank... My pleas to Will to please eat something mix with his stubborn refusal to taste his oats and Jo's protests her favorite cereal are over. On top of that, Bram's wailing because I'm not keeping him in my arms while trying to deal with all of this. And even the house cat—turns out Mr. Whiskers-Winkle is our cat—is against me and vomits on the kitchen floor.

Sam asked me if I could handle stuff on my own for fifteen minutes, and I naively said yes. But when he comes into the kitchen to a scene of total chaos, my husband takes the situation into his hands at once.

He convinces Jo she can survive on regular Krispies for one morning, remakes Will's oats in the appropriate consistency mixing in the proper amount of apple purée, and gives the cat the right hairball care chews so that he won't hack and gag in distress all over the kitchen floor. In addition to all of this, he manages to remake the coffee while also scrambling our eggs to perfection.

Once we're all fed, Sam says, "I forgot to get the paper from the porch."

"I'll get it," I offer.

"Are you sure because I—" he makes to stand up.

"Stay!" I yell louder than I intended, and then in a softer tone, I add, "I could use the fresh air."

If I don't get out of this house fast, I might have a nervous breakdown. The noise, the mayhem, the complexity of it all are making me dizzy.

I pull on an old pair of Uggs—no, not even Uggs but a knockoff brand with paper-thin soles, and grab a random coat as I blast past the front door, breathing in the morning air.

I close my eyes and visualize my pristine, stainless-steel kitchen in Manhattan, where the only sound is that of my espresso machine grinding coffee and producing the perfect Italian Ristretto. I imagine the white porcelain cup I drink from that I won't have to wash because my cleaning lady will. Then my imagination moves to my precisely organized closet, filled with beautiful, stylish clothes and even better shoes. I picture my underwear drawer brimming with La Perla sets. The last comparison is the most staggering contrast, expensive lace and silk, to the stained, plain-cotton flip bra I'm wearing right now.

I'm getting ready to take a fantasy bath in my indoor Jacuzzi when the insistent sound of a basketball bouncing on the floor and off a metal backboard distracts me from the mirage of my old life. I look to my left where the noise is coming from, but a hedge blocks the view on the lower half of my neighbors' garden. The player remains hidden, I can only see the ball being thrown at the ring and mostly missing the basket.

I'm not sure what prompts me to go investigate, but I move to the other end of the porch and peer over. On the other side of the hedge, in a small, plowed square of concrete in front of the neighbors' garage, a girl seven or eight years old with white-blonde hair is bouncing the ball on the floor.

"Melodie!"

The girl looks up, startled. "Morning, Mrs. Crawley.

Merry Christmas. Do you like my new hoop? I've always wanted to learn how to play basketball."

The dumb act gets even more on my nerves.

"Is the Christmas fantasy over yet?" I snap. "I'm done!"

"Don't you enjoy the holidays, Mrs. Crawley? It's said to be the best time of the year."

"Cut the crap," I hiss. "You know who I am and that I don't belong here. Get me out, I want to go back to my old life."

A sly smile curves Melodie's lips, and she drops the pretense. "Ah, Caroline, ever the impatient." She bounces the ball on the ground, passing it from one hand to the other. "You still need a little time. How's life in the suburbs treating you?"

"Oh, let me see, so far I've been milked worse than a dairy cow, regurgitated on, thrown food at, yelled at, my younger kid can't stay more than half an hour away from me without having an anxiety attack, my middle kid resents me for having had another baby, and my daughter hates me for not buying her a phone when she's not even seven yet. And did you know it's normal for babies to poop up to five times a day? I'm living the life!"

Unperturbed, Melodie keeps smiling and bouncing the ball. "And how's the husband?"

A memory of last night's hot kiss flashes before my eyes, and I can almost feel Sam's lips on my neck and his hands moving down my back, so much that an involuntary shiver runs down my spine. But I recover quickly and snap, "Apparently his sole concern is how soon he can impregnate me again, so I'd say we're even less on the same page than we were seven years ago. Seriously, I never asked for this, I'm ready to go back to the real world. Please tell me what I have to do."

Melodie shrugs. "Sorry, my hands are tied. When you're ready, you'll know."

I'm about to berate her when the front door opens behind me.

"Charlie Bear," Sam calls, then he peeks his head out. "Oh, there you are. I was getting worried, I thought you might have slipped again."

"No, I'm fine, I was just…" I'm about to say I was just talking to the neighbors' kid, but as I glimpse over the hedge, Melodie and the ball are gone. "I mean, I was…"

Sam is by my side in three quick strides. "Are you okay?" He cups my face and looks me in the eyes—more clinical than romantic, as if searching for clues I might drop dead any minute. "The doctor said to call right away if you showed signs of confusion."

"I'm not confused," I say, removing his hands from my face. "I was only checking out the mmm…" I point at the neighbors' house.

"The Bradys' house?" Sam asks.

"Right, the Bradys," I repeat, storing the information. "They've mounted a new basketball hoop just underneath Bram's room. I hope it won't be too loud."

Sam looks over at the neighbors' garage and frowns. "You can't remember the neighbors' name, but you know the hoop is new?"

I shrug and tap my temple. "The information must've been stored in a different compartment."

Sam's features relax. "Okay, it's good you're remembering something, it doesn't matter what. Let's go inside." He puts an arm over my shoulder and steers me toward the door. "Or we're both going to catch a cold."

In the hall, he helps me remove the coat and hangs it on the overstuffed rack mounted on the corridor wall.

"Hey, I was thinking," Sam says. "The bookshop is closed today being Sunday and all. Would you like to go see it? I thought it might be good for your memory and your..." he hesitates.

"My what?"

"Well, your morale."

Apparently, I'm supposed to enjoy myself while I deal with baby poop, cat vomit, soggy oats, and missing cereals... Boo-hoo grumpy me.

"What about the kids?" I ask, sulking even more.

"I texted your mom. She can keep Jo and Will and we'd only have to bring Bram with us, but he's probably going to sleep the entire time."

Having to deal with "just" one kid is better than having to take care of the fool roster, so I promptly agree. Plus, if anything could cheer me up on this crappy day it's a visit to a bookstore, even if I had to give up my publishing company to start it.

"Let me just take a quick shower," I say, pointing at the apple puree staining my T-shirt.

"Okay." Sam kisses me on the forehead. "I'll bring the kids to your mom in the meantime and I'll catch you down here in a bit."

In the shower, I comb the conditioner through my hair. When I finish, I look down at the knot of hair in the bristles, panicking. I remove the excess shedding and pull the shower curtain open to throw it in the toilet. I pass the comb through my locks once more, and again, it comes down loaded with hair. Too much hair. At this rate, I'll go bald.

I throw the second handful of hair in the toilet as well,

just as an unexpected sob shakes my shoulders. Before I know what's happening, I'm standing under the hot water jet, crying like a crazy person. Hard, desperate sobs shake my entire body. I rinse the conditioner away, but as I pass my hands through my scalp, yet more hair falls off.

The hair loss is so upsetting I don't even rinse properly. I hurry out of the shower and sit on the toilet, still crying uncontrollably.

That's how Sam finds me. He comes into the bathroom— I must've forgotten to lock the door, having lived alone for several years I never do it anymore—and reels in shock at the scene before his eyes.

He's by my side at once. "Charlie Bear, what's happened?"

I can't stand to tell my gorgeous husband who, quite unfairly, still has all his beautiful hair that I'm going bald. His attempts to comfort me only make things worse, so I forcefully push him out of the bathroom and lock myself in.

Sam spends a good fifteen minutes knocking and whispering soothing words behind the closed door. Then he must decide he can't handle Crazy Caroline on his own and must go search for help because the bedroom goes quiet.

Alone, I manage to reduce the uncontrollable sobbing to a hiccuping wailing. When a knock comes on the door a while later, I'm almost calm.

"Caroline," Fan says. "What's going on?"

"Is Sam with you?" I wail.

"Yes?" my sister confirms.

"Ask him to leave, I don't want him to hear."

A whispered argument ensues on the other side, and even if I can't see him, I can feel Sam's frustration. But in the end, the bedroom door shuts and Fan says, "We're alone."

"Are you sure?" I ask. "He didn't just pretend to go away and is still next to you listening quietly?"

"No, Caroline. Sam is gone. Now tell me what's happening."

Chest already shaking, I half cry out, "I'm going bald," and begin sobbing again.

"Caroline," Fan says authoritatively. "Stop crying, you're not going bald."

"No, I am, and there's nothing you can do, there's nothing anyone can do."

"Caroline, you just had a baby, a little hair loss is perfectly normal. You're not going bald, I promise!"

"A little hair loss? I'm shedding worse than an Alaskan Malamute, Fan."

"Still normal."

A flicker of hope surfaces in my chest. It gives me enough strength to open the door and talk to Fan face to face.

"Are you sure?"

"Positive." My sister smiles.

"But my hair is falling by the lock, you should've seen. How can it be normal?"

"Do you want the technical explanation?"

"Yes, please."

"Well, your body has been pumped full of estrogens for nine months, preventing your hair from falling throughout the pregnancy. And now that your estrogen levels have dropped, you're shedding your normal quantity plus the nine months of backlog all at once. And you're breastfeeding, so the process is happening faster."

"But will my hair grow back?"

"Totally," Fan announces confidently.

"Ah."

Super relieved, I hug her, and the floodgates open again. "Sorry, I don't know why I can't stop crying."

My sister pats my shoulders affectionately. "Still the hormones."

"Why?" I wail. "Why would any sane woman put herself through this process, and three times no less?" Not to mention the fourth I've already agreed to—*in stone.*

"Come on." Fan squeezes my shoulders and forces me to look at her. "You just had a crash course in all the negatives of motherhood with none of the positives."

"What positives?"

"The overwhelming love you feel for your kids, the way they surprise you every day, the sense of purpose, of fulfillment."

I must look at her with a very dubious expression because she adds, "Wait until Jo tells you something impossibly clever for her age, or for Will to smother you with kisses, or for Bram's first word. Trust me, it's the little moments that make every sacrifice worth it."

I still don't believe her, but I sniffle and nod. "Please go tell Sam I'm not about to have a nervous breakdown and that I'll be down in ten minutes. And, Fan." I take her hands and squeeze them. "Thank you. I've always looked down my nose at you for being"—I make air quotes—"only a stay-at-home mom when I didn't know your job is the hardest in the world."

Fan shakes her head, smiling. "What are you talking about? You never looked down your nose at me, not once in your life."

Oh, Fan, I only wish that were true.

I give her a long, loaded hug and let go only because she has to put Sam out of his misery. "Now go reassure my husband before *he* cracks."

"Yeah," Fan laughs. "Or before my house burns down or something. I left Elijah alone with the fantastic four."

Ten

Memories

As I head downstairs, I'm embarrassed at my quasi meltdown.

Sam is in the living room with his coat already on and with Bram strapped to his chest in a reverse koala position where the baby faces forward. The hubby is holding both of Bram's little hands, waving his arms in a little dance in synchrony with his feet, and humming. Bram is laughing his head off, Sam is smiling, and they're just too cute a sight.

Something must be terribly wrong with me, I've gone soppy, I'm losing my cool because I feel like crying again. To stop the tears, I take a step back up the stairs and consciously inhale. And why is it that even happy moments threaten to have me break down into a sobbing heap?

One, two, three deep, steadying breaths, and I'm ready to enter the living room.

Even if Fan must've already reassured him I'm okay, Sam's eyes light up when he spots me across the room.

"Look who's here," he tells Bram. "Mommy has arrived."

"Dah, dah, dah," Bram agrees.

I go to them. "I'm sorry for freaking out on you and for pushing you away, I was just too embarrassed."

"No worries, Baldy." He ruffles my hair.

"Not funny."

"Too soon?"

I lift on my toes and kiss him on the lips. Bram chuckles, delighted at being squeezed between us, and I kiss him on the head too. There's something about babies' heads that just compels kisses.

"Shall we go?" I ask.

Outside, the sky is ashen and mottled with clouds, and a few lazy snowflakes are drifting down in irregular swirls. The weather is not so bleak that we can't walk, but Sam goes back into the house and carries out a gigantic black umbrella. He checks that Bram's hat is covering the baby's ears, opens the umbrella, and offers me his arm.

The curbs have been plowed, and ours are the first footprints on the thin layer of dusty fluff already covering the cleared path. This is my hometown, but oddly enough, it is Sam now that guides me through its streets, pointing out buildings of interest as we go: Jo's elementary school, Will's kindergarten, our favorite restaurant—a new one that hadn't opened yet when I left for college fifteen years ago, and so on. Until finally, we head up Market Street toward Russell Square.

Sam has chosen the angle of approach so that when we reach the square, the bookshop is standing on the opposite side, giving us a "wide-angle" view of its large windows filled with multicolored books. I stop in my tracks as I see my childhood fantasy materialized before my eyes as if by magic. The shop is where the old Stansfield Pharmacy used to be. Whenever I played librarian as a kid, this is the spot I always pictured.

The store sits on the corner of Russell Square and Greenbrook Road on the ground floor of one of the oldest buildings in town, quaint with its wooden slating and turrets. The main window has maintained the old dark-wood and slightly undulated old-glass paneling original from the time of construction, and the storefront is concave, following the gentle curve of the square. I look up at the name painted on the top wooden panel, scratched and discolored as if it were as old as the rest of the shop.

"Oh my gosh," I gasp. "I called it Rumpelstiltskin Bookshop."

Sam smiles next to me. "You said you wanted an important name, and that Rumpelstiltskin is as familiar with the concept of name importance as it gets."

I'm so eager to get closer to the shop, I jay-walk, cutting across the square. As I glue my nose to the old glass like a toddler would do with a toy store, I recognize most of the novels on display. A few titles I'm a little ashamed to admit are excellent books I passed over in my universe to pursue more lucrative new releases. In fact, none of the books on display are published by Wilkins and Marley. But that's probably because, in this universe, Wilkins and Marley doesn't exist since the Wilkins part is stuck running a small-town bookshop. But the novels ought to have been written and then published by someone else, which makes me wonder why none of them made the cut to be in the window.

After scanning the covers, I take in the rest of the display, the old-fashioned Christmas decorations, and the faux-snow bedding. It's beautiful.

I wait impatiently for Sam to arrive with the keys. He unlocks the front door and holds it open for me, making the small bell atop jingle.

Hesitant now and a little overwhelmed, I step in. The wooden paneling inside is original from the old pharmacy but stocked with books instead of vials and potions. The registry is where the old counter used to be, while the rest of the space is a maze of tall bookshelves crammed with so many books, books, books. A jigsaw of colored rugs covers every inch of the original hardwood floors. The rugs have rich colors that make the interior glow with coziness despite the gray sky and falling snow.

Whereas the wood paneling is as dark as it was a century ago, the bookcases installed in the middle are painted in the same rich colors as the rugs.

The store is a mix between an old library and a Middle Eastern bazaar, and I love it.

I move through the shelves, entranced, running a finger across the spines, smiling at certain books as if I was being reunited with old friends. I move across the wilderness of genres: poetry, classics, romance, history, travels, mystery, fantasy, children's books. You name it, the shop has it. Cozy armchairs are scattered around to allow customers to sit awhile and read. In the back, a miniature café is surrounded by chairs and tables and, best of all, a colossal fireplace, with an antique white marble mantelpiece. The wall above is decorated with mosaic tiles in the same colors as the rugs. At first, the tiles appear to form a random arrangement of colors, but as I step in front of the fireplace and take a few steps back to see the complete picture, I gasp in delight once again. At once, I recognize Sam's artistry in a reproduction of my favorite scene from *Little Women*. The one where the girls wake up on Christmas morning to find books concealed under their pillows as their sole present for that year. Jo is holding a red book, and Meg with a green one, Beth with a blue book, and Amy, gray. The sky is "rosy with the coming day" just as in the book.

I turn around to go find Sam and bump into him and Bram already standing behind me.

"You made that!" I say. "It must've taken you forever."

I realize now with shame that when Sam told me about

94

our third mortgage being for his studio, I didn't even ask about his work. I was too absorbed in the revelation of being a small-time bookshop owner instead of a powerhouse publisher.

"You started a mosaic business as you've always wanted," I say.

Sam inches his chin at the mosaic. "Yep, we're both doing our dream job."

"And mosaics pay the bills?" I ask, bewildered.

Sam shrugs. "Some years are better than others, but we make a good living."

A suspicion tarnishes my good mood. "Has your business been supplementing mine?"

"No, honey, the shop is very successful. The business stands on its own."

"Then why are we so strapped for money? Why don't we have a nanny?"

Sam laughs. "A nanny? You? You're so jealous of your kids you have trouble leaving them with a babysitter for one night, let alone a nanny. Trust me, you're not the nanny type."

That doesn't sound like me at all, but I refrain from commenting.

I'm about to go explore a little further when Bram starts to fuss. Sam takes him out of the sling and pragmatically smells his bottom. "Nope," he says. "He must be hungry."

"Do we have time to go back home or do I have to feed him here?" I ask, looking dubiously at the reading armchairs. Will they be comfortable enough for breastfeeding?

Sam's lips curl in an enigmatic little grin. "Mrs. Crawley, please follow me."

He guides me down a short corridor further to the back of

the store, to what must've been the old pharmacy's storage room. Sam opens a door and flips on the lights. Then he gestures for me to remove my shoes, doing the same, and guides me into an airy room decorated in pastel tones. A blue sky is painted on the ceiling, dotted with white fluffy clouds, and on the walls, various scenes from *The Tale of Peter Rabbit* by Beatrix Potter.

I turn to my husband. "Did you paint this, too?"

Sam nods.

"What is this room?" I ask.

"Mommies' Heaven, a space you set up where moms can come and feed their babies in a separate room, talk, and," he points at the light-wood bookcases, "of course, buy books on every topic ever written on motherhood."

I study the room more in depth, besides the four large rocking chairs, and scattered toys on the floor, the shelves brim with instructional manuals. From the obvious *What to Expect When You're Expecting,* to breastfeeding guides, books on self-weaning, potty training, sleep training, and all other parenting topics. I check out a few titles: *Mommy Burnout; Breathe, Mama, Breathe*—I ought to read these two. Then I pick up an orange paperback whose title makes me arch an eyebrow: *How Not to Hate Your Husband After Kids.*

I show the book to Sam. "Is this a thing?"

He chuckles mysteriously. "Let's say we've had an adjustment period after Jo was born, and, yes, you've made me read it." Sam smirks in that irresistible way of his. "I'm a good boy now."

Bram lets out an indignant scream at being ignored. I exchange the paperback for my son and sit in one of the rocking chairs. I fumble with my clothes as per the usual unbuttoning, shifting of secret pockets, and opening of secret bra flaps and give the little mothersucker his breast.

Sam replaces the book on its shelf and sits across from me.

"I'm usually not allowed in here."

"And how do you feel being one of the mommies?"

Sam smiles and reclines in his armchair. "Pretty great, actually."

A while later, Bram lets go of breast number two and burps and poops at the same time.

I lift the baby and hand him to Sam. "Well, here comes one joy of motherhood for you."

***

That evening we eat Christmas leftovers kindly provided by my mom—thank goodness, as I'm no cook and I doubt Nobu takeout is an option in this zip code or on this household's budget.

Afterward, Sam offers to put the kids to bed and I gladly accept. I go lie on the couch in a rare moment of silence. Unable to relax, I stare at the ceiling filled with dread for tomorrow when Sam will go to work and I'll be left alone with the three little monsters. He warned me the next couple of weeks won't be indicative of our usual setup, not with Jo's school and Will's kindergarten both being closed for winter break.

"It's going to be harder than usual, but it's manageable," Sam explained, his words tinged with an ill-concealed undertone of anxiety that basically told me I'm toast.

My good husband offered to stay back and help, even if his jaw kept twitching with anxiety. After some prodding, I wrestled out of him that he is five days away from the inauguration of a new hotel he's designed murals for and really can't be staying home helping me.

After a few more protests, Sam accepted my refusal and told me my mom would do her best to help. Now I see why my sister may have a point in living next door to Mom and Dad.

Sam comes down the stairs now, after using his magical powers to put the kids to sleep, and sits at the other end of the couch. He lifts my legs on his lap, grabbing my ankles for a rub.

I close my eyes and recline my head on the armrest. I'm in heaven.

"That good, uh?" he jokes.

I hum. "You're hired as my personal masseuse. You can never let my feet out of your hands."

"Sorry, but I'm heading to bed soon, early rise tomorrow."

"How come?"

"I have to go to the Koi," he says, mentioning the hotel he's working at. "To supervise the finishing touches on the foyer mosaic, this week's going to be hectic before the grand opening on Friday."

"I can't wait to see the design," I say, remembering Sam wouldn't let me see even a sketch before one of his masterpieces was completed. "I'm sure it'll be fabulous."

Sam gets up and kisses me on the forehead.

"Hey, I found this under the bed upstairs." He reaches into his sweatpants pocket and takes out a phone. "Battery's dead, though."

"Is this my phone?"

"Yep, the charger's right behind you. Are you coming up to bed?"

I cradle the phone in my hands, eager to spy on the life of this alternative version of myself.

"I'll just have a quick look and I'll be up in a minute."

Sam kisses me on the forehead. "Okay, good night, baby." Halfway to the stairs, Sam stops and turns to me. "Oh, the passcode is 1234."

Ah, we're one of those couples who know each other's passwords.

I wait until Sam's footsteps have reached the landing to plug in the charger and wait with a trembling heart for the phone's screen to light up.

1234, and I'm in. The home screen is littered with the standard apps: camera, calendar, mail, contacts, Instagram, Facebook, Twitter, settings, clock, maps, a bank app, period tracking, and a purple ominous What to Expect, which apparently, I haven't deleted after Bram because we're not done having kids.

I've always been a visual person, so I open Instagram first. My handle is @RumpelstiltskinBookshop, a business account. I scroll both my feed and that of people I'm following and, yep, it's one pretty book picture after the other. I'm a solid bookstagrammer, makes sense. Facebook and Twitter are the same. When I open the photo library app, I almost expect it to be all books as well, but that's where family life comes into focus.

The first picture was taken on December 22nd and is one of me and Will; we both have our faces painted as reindeers with red noses, white contouring around our eyes, and we're wearing matching antler headbands.

I scroll back and find mostly pics of the kids engaged in various activities: running, playing, making angels in the snow, eating, sleeping. There are some hilarious ones of

Bram and Will crying and scrunching their faces in the most ridiculous pouts. Jersey Caroline appears in a few selfies and in every single photo, she's smiling. Even in the video where Will is making a tantrum about eating, she laughs as he takes a stand about not eating his vegetables. My skin crawls at the idea I'll have to feed the brat three times tomorrow all on my own. What humor she found in the hissy fit is beyond my comprehension.

I keep leafing through the photos and find one of Sam sleeping in our bed, submersed in a mound of kids. All three are on top of him napping in the billowy blankets. Sweet.

I scroll down to see our family Halloween portrait. Jersey Caroline is a witch with white and red striped stockings, curly pointed shoes, and a witch hat. Jo is dressed similarly, but her stockings are white and purple. Sam is a vampire and the personification of how I imagined Eric Northman the first time I read *True Blood,* tall, irresistible, deadly handsome— no matter that his fangs are visibly rubber gum and that he's the dark-haired, brown-eyed version. Will is a cute mini zombie, and Bram is wearing a wolf onesie, which I suppose makes him the family's werewolf.

I scroll even further into the past and stop when I find a picture of Jersey Caroline at the hospital, she's holding Bram in her arms and looks tired but beautiful, exhausted and ecstatic, sporting a smile as intimate and secretive as the Mona Lisa. Motherhood summed up in a picture full of joy and pain and contradictions.

I continue the stalking of myself, watching in wonder at my nine-month pregnant self. I'm the size of a small whale, as far away from a size four as I've been in my entire life, and yet so beautiful.

I go back in time with the pictures until it's just Sam and

me—no kids.

The first wedding photo catches me by surprise and almost gives me a heart attack. We're on a beach somewhere exotic. In front of a rudimental gazebo made of three sun-bleached wooden poles tied together and decorated with white flowers and with white veils floating in the wind. I'm wearing a simple white silk dress that reaches to my bare feet. My hair is up, collected on one side with a giant white flower. Sam is wearing a white linen shirt and pants and is barefoot, too.

In the picture, we're clasping hands, staring into each other's eyes. The minister must've just reached the "you may kiss the bride" part, because it sure looks like we're about to kiss.

We—*they* look so happy.

My pulse gets slightly tachycardic and I have to lower the phone and go to the kitchen to grab a glass of water. I'm not even sure what's making me anxious, that I might be stuck in this life forever, or that I might have to go back.

I splash my face with water and, once I'm calm enough, I go back to the couch. The photo is still there waiting for me. The date stamped above the pic informs me it was taken on February 22nd. In this life, we got married two months after we broke up in reality. I must've already been pregnant with Jo even if the bump didn't show yet. I wonder why I stopped taking the pill in this world. Did I just give in to Sam's demands or was it my decision, too?

I scroll through the wedding pictures, drinking them in. The sun. The beach. I can almost feel the sea breeze on my face and the sand between my toes, and the warmth of Sam's love surrounding me, engulfing me in a warm embrace

I've scrolled through seven years of life together, and the

sum of it all is that I look disgustingly happy year in, year out.

This isn't real, I repeat to myself.

Real people are never that happy. Such contentment is relegated to family commercials and Hallmark movies. And Jersey Caroline's smiles must be as fake as those *As Seen on TV* ads.

I leave the phone on the couch, plugged into its charger, and tiptoe upstairs.

In the bedroom, I stop at the edge of the bed and watch Sam sleep. I don't care if it's wrong or if I'm not supposed to. I scoot under the covers with him and mold my front to his back. Sam stirs without waking up and takes my arm under his.

Not real, I repeat one last time before falling asleep.

Eleven

Forget about Prince Charming

If, in the night's quiet, having a fake family and a loving husband had an appeal, the next morning brings me squarely back into a, "I'm having my tubes closed" attitude.

Sam gets up with Bram's first feeding at six a.m. and skips breakfast in favor of a travel mug of coffee. Before leaving, he kisses me on the forehead and asks again if I'll be okay on my own.

And since I've always been more proud than practical, I tell him to go, no problem.

Once Bram falls asleep, I attempt to mimic yesterday's routine by bringing him downstairs with me and setting him in his crib. Of course, the mothersucker wakes up the second I put him down and starts crying, lifting his arms to be picked up. I bargain with him to no avail, it's either hold him or the ear-splitting wails. And I try to move around carrying him under one arm on my hip, but after three minutes my arm is about to fall off, my back is killing me, and I've spilled the coffee three times already trying to pour it in the filter one-handed—at least today I remembered to add water to the tank.

This won't do. I drop Bram in his crib, ignoring the wailing no matter how much my nipples are begging me not to, and search the house for the sling Sam used yesterday. I find it on the rack in the entrance hall and strap it to my chest and back, adjusting the length of the straps to accommodate my tinier body. Once the baby is secured and his weight is evenly distributed, I have two free hands and am able to make coffee. Next, I have to wake up the other two. I go to Jo's room as she seems the easier mark. I shake her awake and kiss her on the forehead.

"Time to get up, honey."

She rubs sleep from her eyes with her fists and sits up on the bed.

"I'll be right down, Mommy."

See, that wasn't so hard.

Next, I venture into Will's room. He takes longer to wake. I have to nag him, kiss him, tickle him, and ultimately, only threatening to leave works. Will kneels on the bed and offers his arms to be picked up.

I oblige him and trudge down the stairs with the two little monkeys hanging from my torso without breaking an ankle. *Results.*

In the kitchen, I've barely secured Will into his highchair when he screams, "Pee, weee, I have to go peee peee."

In a panic, I hurry to unbuckle him and pick him up again. I rush to the downstairs bathroom as fast as I can with a baby strapped to my chest and one in my arms, but there's no potty. I don't care. I lower Will's pants and underpants and sit him on the toilet without letting go of his tiny torso.

"You can pee like the grownups."

Bathroom emergency averted, we go back into the kitchen where Jo has served herself a bowl of milk and is already eating her Cocoa Krispies—promptly re-stoked yesterday.

I kiss her on the head. "Thank goodness for you."

Making Will eat breakfast is the pitiful task I'd expected. I have to remake his oats three times before I get to a consistency the little brat will accept and cut a banana to precisely the right dimension and hand-feed the small cubes to him because he refuses the spoon. By the time the ordeal is over, the kitchen is a mess and I'm utterly exhausted. At least the cat didn't throw up today.

I peek at the clock hanging over the door. Only eight-thirty. How will I make it to the end of the day alive?

"What time does the bookshop open?" I ask Jo.

"Nine-thirty," she says. "But don't worry, Pam always opens up. When we're off school, we usually go at around ten."

Pam. Sam mentioned I have a couple of employees; she must be one.

I stare at the clock again. Ninety minutes to get us to the shop seems doable.

"Okay," I say. "Guess we all need to get dressed and then we can go."

Jo eyes me skeptically. "Mmm, Mom, aren't you loading the dishwasher?"

"Dishwasher, sure."

"Down!" Will orders from the highchair.

"What's the matter now?" I ask.

"He doesn't enjoy being in the highchair."

Is there *anything* he likes? I refrain from asking.

I'm pondering if I can have Will strolling around the kitchen while I clean up when the doorbell rings.

Ignoring the toddler's protests, I leave him in the highchair to go answer the door and find my mom on the doorstep.

In my universe, a surprise visit from my mother would irritate me to no end and immediately spur an interior debate on how fast I could get rid of her. Today, I almost collapse with gratitude at finding her at my door.

I hug her, squashing Bram, still strapped on me, between us. "Oh, thank goodness you came."

Mom makes a mock military salute. "Grandma to the rescue. What do you need me to do?"

I consider the two most imminent tasks: cleaning the kitchen versus washing and dressing the kids. Dirty dishes win over dirty diapers without a contest.

"Could you get the kids dressed?"

"Sure," Mom says.

I hand her Bram and go free Will from the dreaded highchair. With the expert touch of a professional grandma, my mom takes Will's hand and guides him upstairs while keeping Bram on her hip. Guess she's more practiced than me.

"Do you need any help, Mom?" Jo asks. "I can show you how the dishwasher works and where we keep the dish soap."

I'm sure I could've figured it out on my own, but my daughter seems to relish in her housekeeping competence, so I let her teach me and then send her upstairs to get changed.

Forty-five minutes later, my mom presents me with three perfectly washed-up, dressed kids.

I hug her again. "Thanks, Mom, you're a lifesaver."

If any doubts were left, I can now one hundred percent agree with my sister's decision to move back to our hometown to be close to our parents.

"Will you get to work, okay?" Mom asks.

"I can manage five blocks."

"Because Will can stay with me if you want to."

This prompts my middle kid to launch himself at me and cling to one of my legs for dear life. "I want to go with Mommy!"

"Guess that settles it," I say. "Don't worry, Mom, we'll be fine."

As my mom leaves, I consider the best way to safely walk those five blocks. I can keep Bram in the sling like Sam did yesterday, and Jo seems mature enough to trail along on her own. But what of Will? Does he walk or does he have a stroller?

I ask Jo.

"Will and Bram go in the double stroller," she instructs me. "And I help you push."

"And where do we keep the stroller?"

"In the garage."

I put coats on everyone, strap the kids in the stroller, and I suppose we're ready to go.

Except Jo keeps giving me side stares. "Did I forget something, honey?"

"Did you make Will pee?"

"Do I have to *make* him pee?"

"If he doesn't pee before we leave, he'll probably have to go while we're walking and then do it in his pants."

Not a scenario I want to experience. I quickly unstrap Will from the stroller and pick him up. "And how do I *make* him pee?"

"Leave him on the potty until he goes."

"All right, please stay with your brother while we go."

I leave her and Bram in the garage and go back into the house with Will.

I sit him on the downstairs potty, which I discovered is in the half bath, and wait for a good fifteen minutes before anything happens. We could've gotten to the shop already, but I won't discount Jo's wisdom. If she says Will has to pee before we leave the house, then he has to pee before we leave the house.

When I get back to the garage, I find my daughter pushing her brother in circles around the room.

"Bram was crying," she explains. "So, I put him to sleep."

For a quasi-seven-year-old, she's extremely mature.

I kiss her on the head. "You're an angel."

"Angel, too," Will protests.

"Yes, you're an angel, too," I say and kiss him even if I'm not entirely convinced of his angelhood.

"Can we go now?" I ask. "Or did I forget something else?"

"Did you take Bram's bag, in case he poops himself?"

I did not.

Once again, I go back into the house to retrieve the bag, and, finally, we're good to go.

At ten on the dot and not a minute earlier, we push our way into the shop, prompting the bell over the door to announce our arrival.

A blonde young woman who, if I had to describe, I'd say is a doppelgänger of Anita in the *101 Dalmatians* cartoon, rushes to welcome us.

"Caroline, you made it. I couldn't wait to tell you about this idea I've had for next month's book club. Can I take the lead on that? Or you had something already in mind? Oh, and the administrative software has frozen again this morning, and I had to input half of January's orders manually. My hand is cramping from all that typing. We should upgrade. On the positive side, Ingram's delivery has arrived. And we might've gone a little over the top with the new inventory, but the amount of sensational new titles." She pauses to sigh and, well, *breathe,* hopefully, and the onslaught of words resumes immediately after. "But I agree we couldn't pass on any of those wonderful books. Do you want to stock the shelves and I man the shop, or would you like me to do the stocking? Or split in half? If you want to split, I call shotgun on fantasy and young adult."

I blink at her in shock, not even sure of how many questions she's asked me.

"Uh? Caroline?" Pam—this must be Pam—says.

"I guess no one's told you," I say.

"Told me what?"

"I had a bit of an accident on Christmas Eve."

She gasps, bringing her hands over her heart. "Oh my gosh, are you alright?"

"Mostly," I say, and then I get closer to her to whisper in her ear so that Will won't hear me. "But I have a bad case of post-traumatic amnesia. The last seven years of my life, poof, have gone. Will doesn't know, so please, no mention of the A-word in front of him."

For a moment Pam is too shocked to speak, which must be an accomplishment on its own.

Then she stutters, "But—but we didn't know each other seven years ago. You've no idea who I am?"

"You're Pam, the shop clerk, or so I've been told."

"Oh." Her face falls as if I've just majorly downplayed her role in my life, which I probably have.

"FREEE!" Will screams from the stroller.

I've noticed he's a selective talker. Sometimes he talks in articulate, full sentences, and at other times, he reverts to single-word phrases. Before he wakes Bram with another scream, I oblige his request, unbuckling his belt and dropping him on the floor.

Will's feet have barely touched the rugs that he's already meandering through the bookshelves heading for a specific section of the store.

"Where is he going?" I ask.

"Epic Fantasy aisle," Pam says.

That seems like an odd choice for a toddler. "Why?"

"He likes to build railroads and bridges with thick books."

I park the stroller behind the counter and follow in Will's steps.

He's already at work, freeing the bottom shelf of all its books.

"And we let him?"

"Oh, yeah," Pam says. "Consider it an alternative display. Customers love watching him play, and often end up picking up a book, especially women." Pam puts her hand partially over her mouth as if to speak in my ear. "Honestly, it's one of the few proven strategies to get rid of the non-sellers."

I'm about to reply when something brushes against my legs, making me jump with a yelp. An extraordinarily fat cat is brushing against my calves.

"There's a cat. What's a cat doing in the shop?"

Pam bends down to pick the furry monster up. "This is Winston." She waves one of his paws in greeting. "The shop cat."

"As in he lives here? He wasn't here yesterday."

"Well, no. I take him home with me when I go at night, but he likes to spend his days here."

"So, you mean he's really *your* cat that you bring to work." I pause, bewildered. "Why?"

"Well, because he likes it, and customers love him." She nuzzles his head. "And it'd be just plain mean to leave him home all alone all day long."

The cat meows in agreement and bumps his head under Pam's chin.

"Should I have brought Mr. Winkle-whiskers?" I ask, thinking of my cat alone all day. Did Jo forget to tell me?

Pam shakes her head decisively. "Nooo, nope, no. They're sworn enemies."

"And my cat doesn't suffer being home alone all day?"

"Mr. Winkle-whiskers is more of a free spirit, and if he feels alone, he can always visit your mom or your sister. Plus, he doesn't like the shop as much as Winston and isn't as well behaved." Pam scratches her cat behind the ears. "You're such a good boy, aren't you?"

The cat gives her another chin bump and then tries to get free.

She lets Winston down, but instead of scurrying away, the brown and gray cat lifts on his hind legs, placing his front paws on my thighs.

"What does he want?" I ask.

"He wants you to pick him up. He hasn't seen you in two days and he misses you."

I pick up Winston, who weighs more than Bram, and hold him awkwardly in my arms. He purrs all the same.

"We get along?"

"Perfectly."

"And he doesn't sharpen his claws on the books?"

"Nooo, he's very well trained and uses his cat tree by the café for that. He spends most of his time there being petted by patrons."

"Mom." Jo tugs on my sweater. "Can I bring Winston to the fairy tale section with me?"

"Sure, honey."

I hand over the cat, check one last time that Will is doing okay—he seems taken with his construction work, and ask Pam to show me the ropes of how the shop runs. From basic stuff like how the registry works, to our stocking system and how we run the café—apparently whichever one of us is free also serves coffee and pastries to clients.

Bram wakes up after an hour, I feed him in the mommies' room and change his diaper alone for the first time. Thankfully, there's no poop spillage and I don't have to remove all his clothes but just the diaper. The result is a little lopsided, but for a first-timer, I'm proud of myself.

Before I know it, it's already midday and time to go home to feed the other two kids and myself. Pam told me I hired a new junior clerk, Elsie, after having Bram, and I want to leave before she arrives. I don't care to explain the whole amnesia business twice in one morning, so I've asked Pam to please bring Elsie up to speed before going on her lunch break.

With some protests, I convince Will to help me put back the books on their shelf with the promise that he can resume his civil engineering later. I secure him and Bram in the stroller and go fetch Jo in the fairy tale aisle. She's sitting on the rugs, back leaning against a bookcase, deeply immersed in a book.

"Honey, it's time to go home," I tell her.

"Can I read for another ten minutes?"

I shake my head. "It's late already."

"But, Mom, Prince Charming is about to wake up Snow White with a true love's kiss."

I refrain from telling her that instead of wasting her dreams on Prince Charming she should focus on the animals that clean the house. What would I give now for laundering squirrels, tidying birds, and cooking rabbits... ah, a girl can dream.

"You can finish the story this afternoon."

"But what if someone buys the book while I'm gone?"

"Let's put it in the back," I say with a cheeky grin. "That way no one will find it."

We hide the book behind a stash of other titles and I finally have all three kids ready to go.

Twelve

So I Keep Hearing

At home, I still have enough Christmas leftovers not to worry about cooking. I reheat the food in the microwave and serve Jo first. Bram for once is happy playing in his crib and not being in my arms, which leaves me free to fight with Will to make him eat his figurative vegetables. From his highchair, he stares at me as I approach with his warm plate like the evil character of a Western movie who's waiting to draw his gun.

A fiery battle of swatted spoons ensues.

By the time Jo is done eating, I've reached the point of despair. Will hasn't eaten a single spoonful.

My daughter stares at me with almost pity in her eyes.

"Do you know any tricks to make him eat?" I ask.

Jo studies me for a second. "Well, there could be one, but you're really opposed to it."

Hope blooms in my chest. "If it works, why should I be against it?"

"You say it's bad for our upbringing. You and Dad are against letting us watch TV, especially during meals."

Right about now I'd sell my soul to the devil to make Will eat, so TV seems like the lesser evil.

I re-heat his food that has gone stone cold, warm plate or not, and turn on the TV.

"Any program he enjoys watching?"

"The Netflix show with the puffins is his favorite."

I give Jo the remote. "Can you pull it up?"

"Sure."

With the competent push of a few buttons, Jo has the TV on. An episode begins to play, and Will is so taken with Oona and Baba's adventures he doesn't even notice when I bring the spoon to his mouth. He opens up and swallows like a robot. The magic lasts about ten minutes before he pushes my hand away with a decisive, "No."

I look at Jo. "What now?"

"You have to threaten him, put the cartoon on pause until he eats again. But I should say you and Dad really disapprove of this kind of tactic. You say bribes and blackmail aren't sustainable in the long term."

"Pffff, blackmail. This is survival, your brother needs to eat. It's a necessary means for the greater good."

"Okay," Jo says. "I won't tell anyone. But Mom, do you think it'd be possible to return the dress Daddy bought me for Sarah McMullen's party and get the one I really wanted?"

Juggling remote and spoon, I take a good look at my daughter. Jo basically sold me her silence on my TV transgression in exchange for a new dress. She's been subtle and delicate with her request, but laced it with a veiled threat. And since I've just said blackmail is okay to use, I can't even call her out on it. Nicely done, kiddo. She'll be a talented business woman when she grows up.

"What's wrong with the dress Dad bought you?" I ask to better understand the situation.

"It isn't special."

"And why didn't he buy you the other one?"

Jo pouts. "Dad said it was too expensive."

I pause the TV, waiting for Will to open his mouth and restart it when he does. "How much more money are we talking about?"

"Thirty bucks."

The amount seems so ridiculously low to me, but I still haven't gathered how bad our finances are with three mortgages and three college funds to sustain.

"How long before you go back to school?" I ask.

"Two weeks."

I should be long gone by then, but I hope the real Jersey Caroline won't be too displeased with the arrangement I'm about to propose. "How about I make you a deal?"

"What kind of deal?"

"Today you've been very supportive in helping me get a hang of things, I'd like to hire you as my PA."

"What's a PA?"

"A personal assistant. The pay is two dollars a day, times two weeks it should cover the difference."

"The minimum wage in New Jersey is 4.13$ *an hour* and I don't even get tips."

A smile tugs at my lips, but I fight hard not to let it show. I've no clue where Jo gets her stats, but she's a bright young girl.

"Well, sorry, this is a take it or leave it kind of deal. Do you want that dress or not?"

"Yes."

"Then you're hired."

When Will finally finishes his food, I put his plate in the sink and turn to Jo. "What now?"

"Brush his teeth and put him to sleep. I can stay down with Bram until you're done." She shrugs, bored. "Grandma should arrive soon."

"Okay, so how does the afternoon work?"

"Will stays with Grandma and we go back to the shop."

I pick up Will from his highchair, he's already rubbing his eyes with his fists. "Do I have a particular technique to make him sleep?"

"Read *The Very Hungry Caterpillar* to him, he won't listen to any other story."

Washing a toddler's teeth is another experience I could've done without in my portfolio. At least the hungry caterpillar delivers on his promises and does a quick job of making Will fall asleep.

I have to confess that watching him sleep in his tiny bed with his arms up next to his face—the same position Sam sleeps in—he's really sweet. I kiss his soft, puffy cheek and leave the room.

After my mom arrives, Jo, Bram, and I get ready to go back to the shop.

"You can use the single stroller now, Mom," Jo instructs me. "And I brought my dress to exchange at the store."

"Shouldn't you earn the money first, and then exchange the dress?"

"No, the party is next Saturday. I need an advance on my salary." And before I can counter, she adds, "Trust me, Mom, I won't let you down."

I'm sold. I ask her to show me where to find the single stroller, strap Bram in, hang her cellophaned dress on the handle, and we're ready to go.

At work, Jo goes right back to her fairy tale while I meet my other employee, Elsie, who's very empathic in her discretion and doesn't ask a single personal question.

Unfortunately, ten minutes later, I can't avoid bumping into a customer who thinks she knows me and have to explain the situation to the sweet old lady, who probably has nothing better to do than ask me too many questions about the amnesia. The conversation requires more energy than I've left after the lunch break.

Once the elderly lady has been dispatched, I'm more than ready to go hide in a corner and never come out.

I'm quietly heading for the privacy of the office to hole up for the rest of the afternoon, pushing Bram's stroller along, when Pam steps in front of me fidgeting, fretting to say something.

"What is it?" I ask.

"This week's newsletter, we ought to send it and pick a read for January's book club…" She shares a guilty stare with Elsie, who's manning the café.

"And?" I prompt.

"Well, Elsie and I have been thinking we should have an amnesia-themed month, if that's not too insensitive to you. Amnesia is a popular romance trope, and the book club would enjoy a lighter read for a change." One thing I've already picked up about Pam is that once she's on a roll talking, there's no point trying to stop her so I let her finish. "But usually February is our romance month, so we would also have to explain what happened to you when we put the book forward, which could be a good thing as you wouldn't have to repeat the story to every single patron you don't recognize. But it could also backfire…"

"How?"

"You know how people are, nothing ever happens in this town, and once the word is out you have amnesia, a bunch of busybodies could pop into the shop just to snoop."

I cross my arms on my chest. "I'd rather deal with a few curious customers than having to explain a million times why I can't remember anything of the past seven years."

"Great, then that's settled."

"Have you already picked a book for the club?"

Elsie replies before Pam has a chance. "We were

undecided between a lighter *Remember Me?* by Sophie Kinsella and a nonfiction title, *The Vow,* the Carpenters' true story. That couple's story is so similar to yours, but at least you remember being with Sam, even if you don't recall marrying him."

Because it didn't happen, I want to say. But I keep my reply practical instead. "Why don't we let the book club decide? Can we put a poll in the newsletter?"

"I'll set it up in our Goodreads group so I can pick a definitive end date for it. We need to account for enough time to stock the book."

"Sounds like a plan."

I finally make it to the office and shut myself in with the baby. For the first ten minutes, I relish in the quiet. In the next ten, I organize the desk. By the half an hour mark, I'm already bored to death.

I even peek at Bram hoping he might give signs of awakening, but he lets out a peaceful, bubbly snore in reply.

Resigned to the need for human interaction, I exit the room and ask Pam to show me our method to stock the shelves. She gave me a rough idea this morning, but nothing beats a practical lesson.

I help her carry up the boxes of new arrivals from the basement, and we set up a little sorting area in the faraway corner of the shop where we won't be bothering patrons.

As I open the first box, I can hardly contain my excitement at the treasures hidden underneath. Each book is a unique story, a different world, or adventure.

As Pam and I shuffle books out of the boxes and discuss their placement—top, middle, bottom shelf, cover forward, spine only, front table new releases, and the honorary window spots—I can't help but notice again none of the books are from Marley Press. Jackie, my partner at Wilkins and Marley in my universe and former colleague in this reality, did leave Bucknam and founded her own publishing house—totally stealing my idea—even in this version of the world. But in this dimension, the company only bears her name. Still, the titles published are eerily the same.

"Pam," I say. "I can't help but notice we don't stock anything from Marley Press, is that intentional?"

Pam makes a gagging noise. "Gwak, you—*we*—hate them, they only publish rubbish with no spine—pun intended."

Despite myself, I blush. "Oh. But surely we can find at least *one* quality book in their catalog?"

"Not a one, trust me. You always tell me they're everything that's wrong with publishing."

Mortified, I'm scrambling to come up with a reply when an ear-splitting, high-pitched wail rips through the store.

Saved by the baby!

"Guess someone's hungry," I say, leaving the last few books for Pam to sort alone.

I free Bram from the stroller and retire to Mommies' Heaven to nurse him. While the little mothersucker goes to town on my breasts, I reflect on what Pam just told me. I keep hearing Yashika's voice as she begged me to publish a—frankly stellar—novel and me refusing in favor of publishing yet another empty, ghostwritten celebrity memoir. True, the company I built in my other life makes money by the bucket, but at what price? And couldn't we make the same if not more publishing worthy stories?

When Bram is done eating, I ask Jo if she can play with him for a while. She's started another fairy tale and looks like she has a mind to say no. Then she must remember her support isn't voluntary anymore and that if she wants her new dress, she has to work for it because Jo reluctantly drops her book and goes to Mommies' Heaven with her brother while I stalk Pam around the shop.

My clerk is helping a middle-aged woman choose her next great romance with the competence and enthusiasm of a real booklover who clearly enjoys her work. Once she's shipped the customer out of the store with a stack of shiny new paperbacks, I corner her behind the counter.

"Pam, can you show me the store's books?"

"Oh," she yelps, and jumps back, frightened. "Caroline, you scared me." She recovers quickly. "You want to see last month's figures or what time frame are we talking about?"

"How quick does our accounting system update?"

"It's basically instantaneous, why?"

"Then can you pull up this year's and last year's balances? With only a few days left in December, it should be an accurate enough number."

"Okay, let me tell Elsie we're going into the office."

A few minutes later Pam brings up the accounting program on the office's computer and with a few expert clicks prints out two reports, which she hands to me.

I stare at the numbers, flabbergasted.

I point at the long string of characters at the bottom of the email. "This is how much we made last year? *Net?*"

"Yes."

"After paying my salary, your salary, Elsie's salary, cost of goods, taxes?"

"Mm-hm."

"Pam, this number is too big. We would have to sell too many books. The store can't physically contain all this paper."

"Well, no, but fifty percent of our profits are from the online store."

"We sell online?"

"Yep."

"And don't shipping fees sink us?"

"No, most of our online sales are for eBooks?"

"eBooks? How is that even possible?"

Pam spends the next twenty minutes explaining our partnership with a major eReader producer and how the move has saved the shop during the Great Pandemic. How people choose to buy from us for the superior quality of our virtual storefront, recommendations, and curated editorial lists. Then she praises my business acumen and basically tells me I'm a luminary.

I'm still too shocked to believe her.

"But if I make this much, plus Sam's income." I don't know how much he makes exactly, but it can't be pennies. "Why do I live like a pauper?"

"What do you mean you live like a pauper?"

"My house is crap, I don't have a nanny, a maid, or a chauffeur, and our car is a minivan, a minivan, for Pete's sake. And all my clothes are rags. You know I don't own a single designer item?"

"Well, my, Caroline, has this amnesia thing given you a princess complex?"

"Why? What's wrong with wanting a few comforts?"

"For one, we aren't in a *Downton Abbey* episode. You'd never want a nanny to raise your kids."

So I keep hearing.

"Maura, the woman who cleans the shop, helps you at the house a few times a week. And you don't need a chauffeur. Where would he even drive you? The five blocks to your house? Which, by the way, is a gorgeous home and not *crap* by any standard."

"It's no Manhattan penthouse, though."

"No, but you wouldn't want Jo, Will, and Bram to grow up in the city. And you drive a minivan because it is one of the few cars that can fit three car seats."

"Okay, but if I don't spend on clothes, cars, or anything else fun, where does the money go?"

Pam shifts on her feet, deeply uncomfortable. "I'm not your personal accountant, but if I had to guess I'd say you have the kids' college funds—"

"Do you know how much those are?"

Still uncomfortable, Pam says, "About fourteen hundred each, I think."

"Per month?" I ask.

Pam nods. "Then there's the mortgage on the shop"—she taps the papers in my hands—"which is not counted here as you wanted to keep the walls and the business separate."

"And how much is that?"

"Twenty-five hundred a month. And the mortgage on the house. Jo goes to a public school, but you're in the best school district in New Jersey so your house must've cost a small fortune and the property tax is a bitch."

My head is swirling with possibilities. So far, I'd assumed Jersey Caroline was a business failure, but here she is, sitting on a golden goose and doing nothing about it.

"If the shop is such a success, why have I not made it a franchise?" I fire at Pam, maybe a little too harshly.

She takes a step back and bumps against a cabinet. "You-you meant to, but you wanted things to happen slowly as you needed to find the right partners for every new location?"

"Meaning?"

"Co-owners who are as passionate as you about books and who share the same integrity. I believe you were in talks with five candidates for three new locations in the northeast. You can find everything in your correspondence." She takes another step back as if to leave the room.

A sudden thought occurs to me. "Pam," I stop her.

"Yes?"

"Were we, I mean, are we friends?"

"Yeah, sure, we're great friends."

"So even if I'm your boss you're not terrified of me?"

Pam bites her lower lip. "You're being a little scary right now."

"But I'm usually not."

"No," she confirms. "You're the best boss ever."

"And how does that work with us being friends and me being your boss, too? Do I just let you do whatever you want?" I ask, thinking of the obese cat she brings to work every day.

"Well, you trust my judgment? I guess?"

"And what happens when you screw up?"

"This is a bookshop, not NASA. There isn't much damage I can do... but you're always very understanding even if I mess up."

I consider this statement. "Can you give me an example of a mistake you made, and I didn't berate you for?"

Pam thinks for a second. And just when I'm convinced she's about to bullshit me with an, *I never make mistakes,* she talks, "Like take that time I ordered two hundred copies of *A Court of Mist and Fury* instead of twenty. You didn't get mad at me, you just told me they'd sell eventually and not to worry."

That doesn't sound like me at all. If an employee at

Wilkins and Marley made a mistake that big—comparatively speaking, which would account to making a print order of two hundred thousand copies instead of twenty—I would've fired them without a second thought.

"Did my attitude prompt you to do better in the future?" I ask, genuinely curious.

"Well, yes. I felt so bad for making the mistake that I organized a Night Court-themed costume party with henna tattoo artists and a sort of speed dating area where people could mingle and search for their Fae mate."

"And did it work?"

"Yes, we sold every single copy of the book and gained a lot of new customers. Two of them even got married last year after meeting at our party."

I absorb all this info, digesting it.

Pam must take my silence the wrong way because she says, "Now I'd better go check if Elsie needs my help."

She heads to the door as if she couldn't wait to get away from me, which she probably is.

"Thank you, Pam," I say. "And sorry if I've been a little… intense. It's just that not remembering anything about my life is driving me crazy."

Pam's features soften and a smile comes back to her lips. "I can't imagine what you're going through, glad I could help."

Thirteen

Baby Shark, Tururuduturu

I spend the rest of the afternoon leafing through my emails and computer files with all my plans for the franchising. This is brilliant. If other locations performed like this one, I could replace the loss of Borders, become a household name in book distribution. I could be a millionaire.

I don't know why I'm so excited when, in fact, I already am a multi-millionaire. I'm simply stuck in an alternate reality for reasons still unclear.

A knock on the door interrupts my reverie.

"Mom," Jo pokes her head in, holding her brother in her arms. "Bram is getting restless, he might want to go for a walk, and I've run out of games to make him play. And we need to leave anyway if we want to get to the dress shop before it closes."

I look at the clock mounted on the wall opposite the desk and, oh my gosh, I left my seven-year-old daughter to take care of a baby alone for three hours.

I scramble to get up and relieve her of the chubby mothersucker. Balancing him on one knee, I squat down to be face to face with Jo. "You've been a fantastic assistant today; I couldn't have asked any more of you." I kiss her forehead. "Now let's go shopping."

Jo shows me her brightest smile, tooth gap and all, and I ruffle her hair before getting up.

We leave Pam and Elsie in charge of closing the store, and once on the streets, I awkwardly have to ask Jo for directions since I've no idea where the dress shop is.

Bram enjoys the first five minutes of the change of scenery and then drops sleeping like usual. Strollers are made of magic.

When we enter the boutique, the owner greets us in a tone a few octaves out of a tolerable hearing range.

I must make a terrorized, mommy-who-just-put-her-baby-to-sleep face because next, the owner—a red-haired middle-aged woman with an uncanny resemblance to the actress playing Lilah Folger senior in *Snowpiercer*—starts whispering, "Oh, sorry, I didn't notice little Bram was sleeping."

I must know her well if she's on a first-name basis with my kids. Now the question is, can I fake my way through Jo's dress exchange without having to explain the whole amnesia situation?

"What are you doing back so soon?" Lilah Folger asks—since I don't know her name, that's what I'm going to call her. She bows ever so slightly in Jo's direction. "Is something wrong with your dress, sweetheart?"

"No, Mrs. Parry, but Mom has agreed to buy me the princess gown, the pink one with the tulle skirt."

"Really?" Mrs. Folger aka Parry sends a dubious glimpse my way. "I thought your daddy had ruled it out."

"Yes, but I'm working to earn the difference. Mommy has hired me to be her personal assistant throughout the holidays."

Seeing Jo so proud of her hard work is heartwarming and fills me with pride as well. She's an extraordinary mini-human.

"How wonderful," Mrs. Parry says. "Should I just pack the new dress, or are we trying it on?"

This last question is addressed to me.

"She's trying it on," I say. Mostly because I want to make sure price was the only reason Sam didn't buy Jo the princess gown.

It must've been, because when Jo twirls out of the fitting room, she's a vision. She admires herself from different angles in every mirror in the shop. Jo is so young but already so feminine, and I have to admit the dress is super cute. Flower appliqués cover the bodice, and the blush tulle skirt reaches to her mid-calves.

I give Mrs. Parry a nod and go to pay while Jo gets changed again.

For a moment, as I approach the cashier, I panic. Does Jersey Caroline have enough money? Do I even have my wallet in my bag? I check, and yes, it's there. I take a random credit card out and hand it to Mrs. Parry, following with trepidation as the POS machine processes the payment. When "transaction approved" appears on the screen, I quickly sign the receipt with a sigh of relief.

"Is everything all right, Caroline?" Mrs. Parry asks. "You're awfully quiet today."

Before I can lie with a non-committal I'm fine, Jo rats me out, "Mom has amnesia, she can't remember anything from the past seven years, including having me or Will or Bram, or not even marrying Daddy."

And I want to say the expression on Mrs. Parry's face is pure shock, but I also detect a sort of delighted enjoyment.

"But how is that possible?" she asks, no doubt craving more juicy gossip.

"I slipped on the ice and hit my head, but the doctor says the injury isn't serious and that I should be alright in no time. Now, sorry, but we really have to go," I fake smile, hoping the tidbits of gossip are enough to stifle her interest. "Dinner time."

If nothing else, having kids and schedules to follow is a great excuse to get out of any situation.

***

When we arrive home, Sam hasn't returned yet. Mom hands me a happy Will and informs me they spent the afternoon mostly playing with his toy cars in the bathtub.

"You do smell good," I say, picking up my son. "All fresh and clean."

Now that he is in my arms, Will clings to my neck with the usual desperation. To say goodbye to my mom and thank her, I have to strain my neck to one side while Will struggles to keep me in place.

Once Mom is gone, and Jo disappears upstairs to admire her new dress, and while Bram still sleeps in the stroller, I take a minute to sit with Will and have a chat.

I drop on the couch and convince him to let go of my neck to look me in the eyes.

"What's going on?" I ask.

"Why you don't love me anymore, Mom?"

I might not be the best mother in the world or not have been at the job for long, but even I know how to answer the accusation. "Of course, I love you. What makes you say that?"

"Bram. I hate him."

"No, you don't. He's your brother and one day you'll be best friends. And I spend more time with him only because he's little and can't do anything by himself. Bram isn't a young man like you."

"I still don't like him."

"Don't say that, soon he'll grow up and you'll be able to play together all the time."

"No."

"Come on, you shouldn't be jealous of Bram, he's just a little mothersucker who can't even talk."

Will ponders my statement, serious at first, but then he throws his head backward laughing. "Bram's a mothersucker, I like that, Mom."

On second thoughts, probably it wasn't the best idea to voice my nickname for my youngest aloud. Ah, hell, whatever.

"Shall we go get dinner started?"

"No."

The declaration fills me with dread.

Will's mealtimes are quickly becoming the terror of my days.

In fact, half an hour later, we're engaged in a battle of wills where not even the TV is working.

"Why aren't the puffins doing the trick tonight?"

Jo shrugs. "Try something different."

"Like what?"

"Baby shark!"

"What's a baby shark? He likes shark videos?"

"No, Mom, it's a song."

Jo pulls the video up on YouTube on the TV and Will becomes excited at once. I sneak a few spoonfuls into his mouth, but the song is over too soon.

"What now?"

"Now you have to sing it to him," Jo hesitates, "and Mom?"

"Yes?"

"Are you cooking anything for us? I'm getting hungry."

Fear spider-walks down my spine. I am *not,* in fact, simultaneously feeding the pickiest of picky eaters and cooking dinner for the rest of the family. And we polished the precious Christmas leftovers at lunch.

What now?

Maybe I can't get a Nobu delivery in Jersey, but I can still go with the next best thing.

"Do you like Chinese?" I ask Jo.

Jo's face brightens. "I love Chinese."

"Any good restaurants we can order from nearby?"

"Sure, Mom, give me your phone, I'll pull up the menu."

While I'm busy singing "Baby Shark, Tururuduturu" on repeat, Jo places the order.

Regardless of all the singing, Will only eats half his meal, but at this point, I'm drained. His food has gone stone cold and disgusting again, and I give up.

I've just reached this liberating decision, when Bram wails that he's hungry, too.

I wipe Will's face, put him down from the highchair, and pick up Bram to feed him.

When the food arrives, I've barely finished nursing. I put the baby in the highchair. Bram can't sit straight on his own, yet, but the highchair is snug enough to give him ample support, and he seems to enjoy the different perspective on the world. I fill the tray with toys and Bram plays content, at least for now.

Unfortunately, no matter that my other son hates the highchair, the moment Will spots his brother sitting in it, he screams, "That's mine!" at the top of his lungs and only a promise that he can sit in my lap while I eat quiets him down.

Amidst all the chaos, I pay the delivery guy and take the food, planning to eat it straight out of the cartons as I don't even have the energy to put plates on the table.

But when I get back to the kitchen, Jo has already laid the table for three. Such a small gesture, but one that threatens to make me break down in tears. Oh, gosh. I *hate* hormones.

I thank my daughter and sit.

Will at once reclaims his right to sit in my lap. I pick him up and search the cartons for my noodle soup.

I pour the content into the bowl Jo has laid out for me and start to eat. At my second spoonful, Will sticks his hands in my bowl, steals a noodle, and sucks it up laughing like crazy as the long pasta slaps his chin.

"Good," he proclaims.

"You like noodles?" I ask, delighted, and watch as he steals another one and then another one.

That's self-weaning for you, I cheer inwardly, awarding my sister more wisdom points.

Sam arrives halfway through dinner, and I can hardly contain my joy. "Look," I say. "Will is eating Chinese on his own."

Sam looks perplexed at first, like he might comment about the healthiness of Chinese food for a toddler, but then must think better of it. He greets us all with a kiss and sits next to Jo. "I was really in the mood for Chinese."

After dinner, Sam puts the kids to bed while I wash the dishes. And if someone had told me a week ago, I would've been glad to be washing dishes, I'd have them committed to a mental institution. Of course, I would've thought the alternative task—putting *three* children of mine to bed— equally impossible.

The kitchen only takes fifteen minutes to sort, after which I collapse on the couch. Sam—short for Samaritan—doesn't join me for another forty-five. I'm already half dozing off when he picks up my legs and puts them on his lap.

"Long day, uh?" he asks.

"Yep."

"How did you manage?"

"Pretty well, all considered. We're alive. You? Everything ready for the inauguration?"

"There's still some work to do, but it'll be fixed for Friday."

I don't ask for more details as I know Sam doesn't like to share his art until he deems it absolutely ready and perfect.

"Did you like working at the shop?" he continues.

Contrary to him, I love talking about books. His question gets me started on a roll about my day in literary heaven. All the things I discovered about my own plans for the future and how I might've scared off Pam with my intensity.

"...I wish we could've stayed until closing time," I conclude. "But of course, Will had to eat, and Jo and I had to leave early to go exchange her dress."

"The dress for the first of the year party? Don't tell me she hoodwinked you into getting her the princess tulle gown, that little minx—"

"Give your daughter, *and myself,* some credit," I interrupt. "Jo didn't hoodwink me, she was perfectly straightforward in telling me why you didn't get that dress."

"But if you knew, why did you buy the other one? I know thirty bucks might not seem like a big deal, but it adds up."

"I know," I say, summoning a mental picture of this family's monthly expenses balance sheet I compiled earlier. "And I didn't just *buy* her the dress, I'm making her work for it."

"Work, how?"

"I've hired her as my personal assistant. Today she's been

invaluable. I would've got lost in the minutiae a thousand times if she hadn't explained how things work around here. And you know that she babysat Bram for three full hours this afternoon, completely on her own." Then, before Sam lectures me on how I shouldn't let a seven-year-old care for a baby for that long, I add, "I was in the office studying the franchise numbers and lost track of time."

Sam digests all this information. "I still think she should learn that when we say no, it's no. I don't want her to grow up spoiled."

"And I don't want her to give up on her dreams, I prefer to teach her she can have nice things if she works hard to get them."

I get my feet back from Sam and get up; he's stopped massaging them a while ago anyway. "I'm going to bed, I'm exhausted," I say, a little stiff.

Having kids is already hard enough, but also having to defend my mothering choices with my husband who has been cozily at work all day—because from now on I'm placing all white-collar jobs in the piece-of-cake category compared to motherhood—is beyond my tolerance grade.

Sam looks like he might want to add something, but he thinks better of it and simply wishes me good night. The hubby might be cutting me amnesia slack, or it could be the unspoken "you weren't here so you can't complain" subtext that shuts him up. I'm not sure. But whatever the reason, I'm glad. A fight at the end of a day like today might prompt me to run down the driveway hoping to hit my head again and land myself back in a coma. Now, that'd be restful.

I fight the exhaustion a little longer to take a long hot shower before bed only because I know tomorrow morning, I won't have the time.

By the time I get under the covers, Sam is already tucked in. I'm well prepared to carry my semi-grudge to the morning, but the moment he spoons me, I melt into his arms and pass out.

Fourteen

New York, New York

I welcome the new day feeling slightly less helpless than yesterday. I have to re-do Will's oats only two times and I remember about fifty percent of the things I should bring to work—Jo covers the other half.

Mid-morning, I leave all three kids at the shop, leaving Jo in charge while covertly giving the job to Pam and head to Whole Foods.

After checking out the cooking books section earlier, I'm convinced smart shopping will be my salvation. The various cookbooks were harder for me to decipher than a Cyrillic dictionary. I couldn't understand the name of half the tools mentioned or ingredients, making me even more terrified of cooking from scratch. When a book titled *You Suck at Cooking: The Absurdly Practical Guide to Sucking Slightly Less at Making Food* seems daunting, I should accept my limitations and work with what skills I have. At Wilkins and Marley, knowing when to outsource has been a key aspect of the company's success. And since I can't have a cook or order takeout every day, twice a day without breaking either the bank or my family's health, I've decided to go with the next best option: store-bought, organic, pre-made meals. This alternative won't be cheap either, but it's the best compromise I can reach.

I don't care if Jersey Caroline was a MasterChef. She probably mastered the science of cooking when she had "only" one kid to feed.

The strategy works. Even with my limited kitchen skills, I re-heat the roasted chicken and vegetables I bought for lunch without burning anything. Jo appreciates the healthy but tasteful meal, and even Will eats without being too fussy. Mom arrives as he goes down for his nap, and I go back to the shop with the other two. Every day is the same routine: breakfast, then bookshop. Lunch, bookshop. Dinner, bed. Sam is pulling long hours at work as the inauguration of the hotel draws closer, and I see very little of him. And even when we cross paths, I'm too tired to do much more than wish him good night.

But on Friday, I have something to look forward to. The Koi Hotel is opening its doors for the first time in Soho on New Year's Eve throwing a fancy, no-expenses-spared party. As part of our invitation, Sam and I were delighted to discover we've been granted complimentary use of a suite for tonight. We've hired an overnight babysitter and don't plan to come back until after breakfast. Mom, after going to her own New Year's party in the neighborhood, is sleeping here in case Bram has a major freak out in the middle of the night. The babysitter isn't a stranger, but she's not Mommy or Daddy, and, apparently, when we aren't present, Grandma is the next best thing.

Almost on schedule, I'm showered and pampered. I got my makeup on, my hair is up, and I'm wearing my new, fabulous silk dress. As I check myself out in the mirror, I could pass for the old—or more the *real*—me. For Manhattan Caroline, nightly galas in town were the rule, not the exception.

As I tighten the string of the only decent sandals—black leather with crossover front straps and high heels—I could find in Jersey Caroline's closet, I long for the new pair of

Manolo Blahnik that I'd bought just a few weeks before Melodie shipped me to this life. Velvet pumps with pointed toes, stiletto heels, and the cutest asymmetrical crystal leaf buckle. The Manolos would've been perfect for this dress. And I'm aware sandals are daring for a New Year's party, but the hotel ought to have good heating, and I refuse to wear any of the scratched old pumps I found in the closet.

I tie the last string, stand up, and contemplate the final result. Well, Mama, three kids don't look at all bad on you.

Sam—who's probably used to seeing me in nothing sexier than yoga pants—is about to have a little surprise.

At the thought, my stomach free-falls as my cheeks heat. I'm spending tonight in a hotel room with my husband without the kids around to interrupt...

Sex, which hasn't been an actual option until now, will be on the table. The thought has been at the back of my head all week, more so as the date of our romantic night grew closer.

If the Christmas night's attempt before Bram's interruption was any indication, tonight promises to be great and *complicated.* Sam is not one of the men I'm used to fooling around with in the city. Sex with Sam is bound to be intense, loaded with unresolved feelings on my side, and who knows what expectations on his. Do I even remember what making love to him felt like? Not really, and I'm scared about how powerful the reminder is going to be.

I conjure an image of twenty-something-year-old Sam on top of me, looking at me with nothing but love and desire in his eyes.

"Charlie Bear," Sam's voice drifts up the stairs, interrupting my internal struggle. "Are you ready? We're going to be late if we don't leave soon."

I put on the only decent outerwear I could find at the back

of the closet and rush downstairs. The black wool duster coat isn't exactly evening wear or suited for this outfit, but I can't go out with sandals and without a coat in the middle of winter. My sense of fashion doesn't go that far.

"I'm ready," I say, as my breath catches a little in my throat at seeing Sam in full smoking. Gosh, three kids look good on him, too. I stare, mesmerized.

My school-girl-crushing over my husband thankfully goes unnoticed as he and the babysitter are busy recapping for everything to be in order before we go.

Does she have our numbers and all the info about where we're staying? Yes.

Does she remember what everyone eats for breakfast? Yes.

Know where the cat food is? Yes.

"And did you leave Bram's milk in the usual place?" the babysitter asks Sam, who in turn looks at me.

I blink.

Sam stares at my full breasts peeking out of the unbuttoned coat, but not with the adoring, half-lost expression men usually reserve for women's chest. He's more skeptical—so much for my great expectations of making his jaw drop. Guess that doesn't happen as easily after seven years of marriage and three kids.

"Did you pump?" he asks.

"*Pump?*"

The hubby swats his forehead. "I forgot I have to tell you these things now. You have to pump your breasts and leave some milk for Bram to eat in the morning or if he wakes up. We have some frozen, but he prefers the fresh one. Plus, your breasts might bother you if you don't pump now."

I blink again. "You mean I have to *milk* myself—

literally—like a cow?"

Sam smiles, amused. "Not with your hands, you use the breast pump in your studio upstairs, and you'd better pack it as well and bring it to the hotel in case you need to pump again tomorrow. I can show you how to do it."

I raise my hand to save some of the sexiness in this marriage. "Sam, YouTube was put on this Earth for a reason. I can manage on my own."

I don't care if he's already seen me *pump* a million times, he hasn't seen me-*me* do it. And I'd like to keep some mystery.

Upstairs, I take off the coat and shimmy out of the silk dress to avoid spilling on it.

I also remove my bra, then search for a breast pump tutorial for the model sitting on my desk.

I assemble the various pieces, place the plastic cup on my left breast, and gingerly push the on button.

The pump comes to life and for the first few pumps, nothing happens. The effect is a lot milder compared to a real baby nursing, so I amp the suction to the max level and wait impatiently for something to happen. A few more empty suctions and the familiar rigid nipple sensation arrives and finally, the milk begins to flow. I watch, fascinated, as the transparent cup fills with jets of milk from my nipple.

The novelty wears out quickly and soon the entire operation becomes boring. Until, randomly, my other boob goes rigid as well and spurs milk like a champagne bottle. When Bram feeds, I always wear breastfeeding bras, but tonight is the one night I thought I didn't need a security bra and promptly forgot about the other-boob-will-spill-too chain reaction. I grab a towel to dab the leak. Gosh, breastfeeding is like another full-time job on its own.

Emptying one boob seems to take forever, and another forever to do the other. Sam must be losing his mind. By the time I re-dress and walk downstairs the proud bearer of eight ounces of bottled breastmilk, I find Sam pacing and checking his watch.

I entrust the bottle to the babysitter and smile at my husband. "I'm ready, sorry."

He kisses my head, relieved. "You've nothing to be sorry about. I should've remembered to tell you. I take everything you do for granted, and the amnesia is reminding me just how much."

If I wasn't actually smiling like an idiot, I'd gag for how sweet, and perfect, and unbelievably sensitive he is. I'm sure other husbands would be sulking and complaining about being late, but not Sam. The only flaw he's ever had is his insuppressible desire to reproduce himself, which apparently not even three little buggers have cured.

Mercifully, traffic isn't bad getting to the city. Sam drives us across suburbia in our minivan, and in no time, we're crossing the state border.

I've been gone for only a week, but the moment we emerge from Lincoln Tunnel—on the right side—New York wields its pull on me. Entering the city is enough for me to buzz with energy.

Sam must sense my excitement, because he turns to me and asks, "You still miss it, the city I mean, don't you?"

"Yeah," I nod. "Always."

From the first time I visited, I never imagined myself living anywhere in the world but Manhattan. New York is the city that never sleeps. The place where everything is possible. The tall skyscrapers glitter in the night with a seductive promise, like when you meet the eyes of a handsome stranger in a bar. Anything could happen.

How could Jersey Caroline give it up? How could Sam? He used to love living on this side of the Hudson, too.

"Don't you?" I ask.

Sam pokes my nose. "I know in your mind we're still renting the two-bedroom in Midtown and loving it. And of course, I miss it." Sam stares out of the window. "But we both agreed it was no place to raise children."

"Why not?" I ask. Not in a polemic way, but in a matter-of-fact, what's-wrong-with-raising-kids-in-the-city, plenty-of-people-do-it way.

Sam scoffs. "For once, we could've never afforded the square footage we have in Jersey. Imagine what a house like ours would've cost us in Manhattan."

Probably less than what I paid for my penthouse, I comment bitterly in my head.

Sam must notice my discomfort because he asks, "A penny for your thoughts?"

"I was just thinking that maybe if we'd waited longer to have kids and given our careers more time to pick up, we would've been able to afford the space here."

Sam shrugs. "Or you could be in a dead-end job you hate, slaving away for some big-name publishing mammoth with no soul."

No, I'd be my own boss. Lead a publishing company with my name on the door. And swim in cash a la Scrooge McDuck.

Of course, I can't say any of this. If I told Sam that without kids in the way I would've become super successful, he would dismiss my words as wishful thinking.

"You love your job," he says on the defensive, as if he had to justify to me our life choices.

"I do," I say truthfully. The bookshop has made me reconnect with literature at a visceral level where novels have gone back to being stories instead of a mere profit-and-loss spreadsheet. Because if I'm being honest, that's how I've been running Wilkins and Marley for a few years now, with only the company's bottom line in mind.

The atmosphere in the car is becoming tense, and I would hate for a silly argument to spoil the night, so I heed Melodie's suggestion again and play the amnesia card.

"I know you moved away seven years ago and had your time to say goodbye, but in my head, I was living in Manhattan last week," I say, which isn't even a lie. "Cut me some slack."

"Sorry," Sam says. "I don't know what I'd do if I suddenly woke up married with three kids."

"Oh, shut up." I swat him playfully. "You'd be the happiest dad and husband in the world."

He lets out a goofy smile. "I probably would, and what about you? You like being a mom?"

The question takes me unaware, even more so because the answer isn't a definitive *no*.

"You know, I've only known the kids for a few days, but now I couldn't imagine my life without them. I'm overwhelmed and in over my head most of the time, but it's amazing to see how clever and independent Jo is. Or how imaginative Will can be. And even the little mothersucker is cute."

Sam roars with laughter. "You call our youngest child *the mothersucker?*"

"Well, it's what he is."

Sam chuckles.

"But most of the time, I feel like a navy seal who's been

sent into action with no training."

Sam reaches out and squeezes my thigh. "You're doing an amazing job even without training. The kids love you, I love you, and you're the best mother and wife in the world."

In my alternative universe, I'm used to feeling on top of the world, even if no one ever tells me. Everyone respects me or fears me or admires or envies me. But does anyone *love* me? And why does it have to feel so damn good to be loved?

Fifteen

Sweet, Tender Love

We arrive at the hotel with just enough time to spare to hand our overnight bags to a young bellhop, get a room key, and rush to the hall for the cutting of the ribbon ceremony.

Once the Koi's doors are officially open, I wander the various rooms admiring Sam's work together with the other guests. I'm walking on solid ground, but, watching the walls, I feel as if I were advancing underwater. Every surface glitters and seems to drift around in all shades of blue. Fish and mermaids swim alongside me as I progress through the different common spaces: the hall, breakfast room, spa, and the reception, which Sam has made to appear like a giant coral reef.

I stare at Sam's creations, forcing my jaw not to slack.

"Sam, this is amazing," I say, out of breath. "The drawings are so clear it doesn't even look like tiles... and the water, it looks like it's moving." I turn to him, placing my hands on his chest. "You're a wonder."

He takes one of my hands in his and brings the palm to his lips for a soft kiss. "You're my muse. I could've never done this without you. Well, you and Jo. She insisted I should go with the water theme."

"You had another one in mind?"

"I liked the idea of a tropical jungle as well, but Jo wanted the mermaids—it's her favorite fairytale—and so mermaids it is."

Sam stops a passing server and grabs two flutes of

champagne, handing me one. "Thank you," he says.

"For what?" I ask, bewildered. I had no role in tonight's success.

"Thank you for supporting me when everyone said I was crazy to pursue this career, that I had no chance to support a family with my art." This part is true. When we broke up, he was just starting out. But I've always been on his side about his art; I trusted he could do great things if he put his mind to it. But his parents... gosh, they were so against an artistic career, he had to double-major in Business and Art to appease them. Even if I should thank them as I double majored too, in English Lit and Business, and if not for our common classes, I probably would've never met him.

After college Sam took up a banking job he hated and that his father had forced him to accept. I was the one who encouraged him to turn the tiny second bedroom of our minuscule apartment in Midtown into an art laboratory where he worked any spare minute he had. I also convinced him to quit the bank once he won a contest to do the tile design for the new Second Avenue subway station.

Even when I didn't have a personal chauffeur and still took public transportation, I never got off at that station.

One of my hands is still resting on Sam's chest and he now squeezes it and brings it closer to his heart. "I love you."

The floor disappears from underneath my feet, and I lean on him not to fall flat on my face. Sam's declaration hits me harder than a kick in the gut, sending me simultaneously into ecstasy and panic because, at this exact moment, I realize that in all these years, no matter if I haven't seen him or talked to him or not even looked at his Facebook profile once, I've never stopped loving Sam. Not for one second.

Everything else that I've filled my life with: money,

power, the fancy apartment, the designer clothes... it's all pointless. This new awareness scares me because I know this Sam isn't real. The real Sam isn't my husband, we don't live together in Jersey, and we didn't make three amazing, beautiful little humans that are half me and half him.

The panic takes over and I try to open my mouth to say something, then close it again when nothing comes out.

Sam cups my cheek. "Are you okay?"

"I'm scared," I say.

"Scared of what?"

"That I won't ever remember the past seven years with you," I say, when in reality, I'm terrorized I'll never get to live them. That I've wasted my life in the pursuit of material things that have left me as empty and cold as my perfect penthouse.

Sam looks me straight in the eyes. "If your memories don't come back, we'll make new ones. Together."

That's another thing I'd forgotten about Sam: he's so steady, so calm even in the worst situations. I'm the one who freaks out while he's always been the rock by my side.

"Oh, Sam," I say, still half-choked with emotions. "I love you, too." Then I bury my head in the nook of his neck because I'm still too shy about saying I love you to his face. I fill my nostrils with his scent and press my body against his solid, flat chest.

Eventually, I look up at him, wondering how long we have to stay downstairs and mingle with the guests before we can go back to our room and make love.

Sam's lips curl into that mischievous grin that makes me lose my mind every single time. "Mrs. Crawley," he says. Then lowers his head to whisper in my ear. "You look like someone who wants to bring me upstairs and have her way with me."

I swallow.

To prolong the torture, Sam kisses me on the neck. "We have to wait at least until midnight."

I stare at the big display clock mounted on the stage at the back of the lobby, it's counting down the minutes until midnight and it informs me there's still ninety-seven of the mothersuckers.

***

As the party progresses, I lose count of how many people come up to Sam to compliment him, or shake his hand, or ask for a business card. For all his success, I shamefully can't wait for the in-public part of the night to be over. Sam and I have been eye-flirting across all the pleasantries. And he might've had sex with me just last week, but from the way he's looking at me, he could be the one who's been waiting for seven years.

Another stranger comes up to Sam to compliment the artist, and while they talk shop, I distract myself scanning the other guests' faces for people I might've known as Manhattan Caroline. Instead, I'm surprised to find a disconcerting number of heads turned our way. Or Sam's way, more precisely. Half the women in here are devouring him with their eyes; and how to blame them? He's the most handsome man in the room, and the kindest, sweetest, most attentive, and, if memory serves me well, stellar in bed. How did I ever let him go?

He doesn't even seem to care about all the female attention. If he notices it, he ignores it. Sam only has eyes for me. Even after being married for seven years and having three kids, he looks at me as the day he hit on me for the first time.

The memory of our eyes meeting across Downstein at NYU hits me, how he cheekily asked if he could sit at my table. My heart skips several beats as I remember his smile, and my elation at finally getting the cute guy from my Econ classes to talk to me.

He was fun, brilliant, and so ridiculously good-looking. A few hours was all the time needed for him to get me in bed that same afternoon. I know I might sound cliché now, but I never did that sort of thing with anyone. Before Sam, I was a solid member of the "never put out until the third date" club.

Not with Sam.

Within a couple of hours, we were tearing each other's clothes off in my tiny but private bedroom—at least as private as a room can be in an apartment with thin walls shared by five girls. But we didn't care if the others heard us. We instantly became one of those clueless couples that are so in love they can't see how annoying their PDAs are to the rest of the world. We spent the rest of the school year in a daze together. Either making love or studying for finals and midterms. Since we shared our second major, we could study together for all our Econ classes, or just next to each other when we were doing our humanities coursework.

I chuckle as I remember that time I couldn't make sense of some basic accounting principle and Sam, dead serious, tried to explain the concept to me butt naked. If I couldn't follow before, his guise sure didn't help. He kept repeating that all transactions should be recorded in the accounting periods when they actually occur, rather than in the periods when there are cash flows associated with them and all I could think about were his ripped chest and abs... and when my gaze wandered a little lower—let's just say the explanation was cut short.

"What are you thinking about?"

His warm voice brushes against my neck like an actual caress.

"That time you were trying to explain the accrual principle to me."

We both know how the afternoon ended, and Sam's eyes now go dark with desire. "Well, I was a brilliant teacher. You, on the contrary, were a naughty student if memory serves."

"Mmm, I don't know, Mr. Crawley, if all teachers behaved as you did, where would our education system go?"

"You passed the exam in the end."

"Yep, I did. And strangely, I can still recite the foundation of the accrual basis by heart. You must've made quite an impression."

Our flirting is interrupted by the hotel manager grabbing the microphone and calling for the guests' attention.

"Ladies and gentlemen, with only five minutes to go before midnight, I invite you all to grab a flute of champagne and gather around. Tonight…"

Blah, blah, blah… the speech goes on but I don't pay attention. I concentrate on the giant red shifting numbers of the digital clock mounted at the back of the stage. Just a few more moments, and Sam and I can finally disappear to our suite and have the rest of the night for ourselves.

By the time a server passes our way and offers us two glasses filled with bubbly, the crowd is already chanting, "Ten, nine, eight…"

I look into my husband's eyes for the longest seven seconds of my life until, at the stroke of midnight, he leans over to kiss me. And okay, Jo might've had a point with all the fairy tales she's been reading because if this is how finding Prince Charming feels, I wouldn't trade it for anything in the world—not even the cleaning rabbits.

The kiss is merely a peck on the lips, but Sam's eyes promise so much more as we clink glasses and take a sip of champagne to celebrate the New Year.

The dry wine has barely trickled down my throat when Sam takes the flute out of my hands and drops it on a nearby table.

He places a hand on the small of my back and leans down to whisper, "We can go now." A shiver runs down my spine while goosebumps ride up my arms.

Since my throat is too raspy with desire to reply, I merely nod.

We shuffle through the crowd as discreetly as possible, not meeting anyone's eye so as not to be stopped.

Then we're in the elevator alone and my heart is hammering like a trapped bird.

Once the doors close, we can't keep our hands off each other anymore. I grab my husband by the collar of his shirt and pull him down to me in a passionate kiss. With my other hand, I yank his shirt out of his pants to get to the bare skin of his back. With my dress being a lot skimpier than a tux, Sam doesn't bother for skin-on-skin contact, he simply cups my butt, pulling me to him until the elevator dings open on our floor. Sam grabs my hand and pulls me down the hall as we laugh our heads off like a pair of carefree twenty-somethings. But, even when I was younger, I've never run so fast in heels.

In the room, we make such a quick job of tearing each other's clothes off, it's like a tornado has them picked clean from our bodies.

Then Sam pushes me back on the bed and settles on top of me, biting my earlobe in that way that makes me lose my mind.

That's when disaster strikes. My nipples become rock hard brushing against Sam's chest and before I can shimmy away from underneath him, the milk-works begin. Warm liquid spurs out of my breasts down my sides and on the mattress in a flood.

"Oh my gosh, I'm all wet," I say, dying of embarrassment.

Sam must misinterpret my words because he stops grinding against me to laugh on my clavicle. "Did hitting your head make you start to talk dirty?"

"No, Sam, I'm serious." I push him off. "I'm literally soaked, I'm leaking breast milk all over us and the mattress."

Sam lifts off me to sit on the bed, and I've never felt more vulnerable and grosser in my entire life. And that's when those damn hormones kick in and I can no longer control myself, breaking out in sobs.

"Why is this happening?" I wail. "No baby is crying." I scramble to cover my breasts with the sheets.

Sam scoots next to me. "Don't worry, it's normal."

"How can it be normal?"

"The hormones that control breastfeeding are the same hormones you produce when you have an orgasm. So when you get excited this," he points at my general chest area, "might happen. But it's no big deal." Sam runs a finger down my arms and kisses my neck. "I don't mind."

"But I do." I shoot out of the bed and run into the bathroom shutting myself in. Sex has suddenly become the furthest thing from my mind. I turn the shower to a scorching hot temperature and get underneath. I take my time scrubbing myself free of all the stickiness and then, wrapped in a towel, removing all my makeup. Then I fish the breast pump out of the vanity case and suck all the excess milk out. When I change into clean underwear, I stuff my bra cups with double padding, and I finally feel brave enough to get out of the bathroom.

Sam is waiting for me on the bed, his boxers are back on and he hasn't gone to sleep or pretended to.

"I'm sorry," I say, scooting close to him.

"Nothing to be sorry about," he says. "You reacted the same way the first time this happened after Jo. I keep forgetting this is all new for you."

"This happens with every kid?"

"It's pretty common, yeah."

"How did I overcome the gross-me-out part the other times?"

Sam gives me a wolfish smile. "You got more horny than self-conscious." He points down at his still semi-naked body. "How to blame you?" We both chuckle. "Also, you always wear a bra when we make love while you're breastfeeding and the ladies"—he points at my boobs—"are off-limits."

"Okay," I say, pondering the double-padded bra I'm wearing right now. It should stop any leaks, but I don't know if the "sexy times" mood is irremediably ruined for tonight.

"And you're okay with all this?" I ask, wondering. Sam has always been a breast man. "The milk doesn't put you off?"

"No, it doesn't," he says. "I love you, whichever way. The things your body has to endure. First with pregnancy, then in childbirth, and breastfeeding... I don't know how women do it."

My brain has fixated on the word childbirth, sending a shudder down my spine. I'm sure glad I didn't have to experience that. And for the first time, I wonder what doing it three times did to this body.

"Does sex hurt after giving birth?"

"Not if you wait the right amount of time."

"Which is?"

"Every woman is different, but for us, it's about four to five months."

My eyes boggle. "Five months? And you're okay not having sex for that long?"

"As I said, we men get the easy end of the bargain. And I'd wait for you for a year if that's what it took for you to heal."

He's being impossibly sweet and sensitive and my lower lip begins to tremble in response. Damn hormones. I don't want to cry again.

Before I can shed the first tear, Sam tickles my sides, making me screech, "Stop, stop, what are you doing?"

Sam moves on top of me, holding my wrists over my head in one of his big hands while he tickles me mercilessly with the other. "I figured you were about to be moved to tears by how caring and considerate your husband is, and I really didn't want you to cry again."

If I could swat him, I would. "That's even sweeter, you daft, horrible man."

Even through the tickling, tears sting my eyes. Sam redoubles his efforts and soon I'm too busy begging for mercy to cry.

Sam must realize the danger is over because he relents. Still, he keeps my arms imprisoned above my head, and his other hand, now resting flat on my side, is searing my skin.

He tentatively moves his palm down my ribcage to my thigh and back up. I raise my hips in response, frustrated that I can't grab him and pull him down to me where I need him.

"Sam, please," I beg again and this time it has nothing to do with tickling.

He locks eyes with me. "You're wearing a bra under that T-shirt, aren't you?"

"Double padding."

That's all my husband needs to hear to make sweet, tender love to me all night long.

Sixteen

All I Want for Christmas Is You

Once I've had a taste, I become addicted to making love to Sam. I'm transported back to those early months in our relationship when we couldn't keep our hands off each other.

In my life as Caroline Wilkins the single, multimillionaire power woman, sex was another practicality I had to tend to. Whomever I was doing it with, I wanted only one thing from them: release. And I tried to reach it as quickly and efficiently as I could, impatient to get rid of my companion the moment the deed was accomplished. With Sam, I don't mind if he takes his time with me. In fact, when we take it slowly—mostly at night when the kids are asleep—I relish the journey just as much as the final destination.

Delayed gratification: someone, somewhere, had a point.

Not to discount our daytime quickies, they aren't any less thrilling or exciting or satisfying. Morning, evening, slow, fast, it doesn't matter. I've turned into a stalker. I ambush Sam every chance I get to rip his pants off, and now that he's between jobs and around the house all day, that happens a lot.

Sam needs time between one project and the next to recharge his artistic batteries, so he always schedules two/three-week breaks between jobs. But the Koi Hotel was such a demanding endeavor that he took an entire month off.

And with him at home, my life has gotten a lot easier on the kids' front. Sam's sabbatical couldn't have come at a better time. Whether he stays home with the kids, or comes to the bookshop with us, or takes one or two off my hands, I can finally breathe. And, compared to when we lived together after college, he's stepped up his house chores game a lot too.

When the holidays end, life improves further. With two kids in school out of three, I feel like being on vacation. I'm rested, energetic, and sated—I won't pretend all the sex isn't a huge mood booster. And even when Sam has to begin the design phase for his new commission, I've got enough of a grip on this mommy and wifey life to handle daily struggles like a pro.

On the first Wednesday Sam is back to work, early in February, he jumps up in bed at five in the morning with a sudden inspiration for his new project—a spa center that asked him to decorate the pool area like an ancient Roman thermal bath. I'm awake as well, since Bram demanded his morning feeding earlier than usual. I didn't feel like sitting in the nursing chair, so I brought the mothersucker back to bed with me.

Sam, as excited as a kid on Christmas Eve, pulls up his pants, hopping from foot to foot as he rambles about nymphs and fauns. When he's fully dressed, with clothes that don't match at all—sweatpants, a button-down white shirt, and an ugly Christmas sweater that somehow escaped laundry day yesterday, he comes over to the bed and smacks his lips on my forehead.

"Sorry, Charlie Bear, I need to get this image out of my head before I forget it. I'm probably gonna be drawing all day, but I'll be back in time for dinner. Are you good?"

"Yeah, honey, you go do your thing, I can take care of the fort," I say, confident I'm telling the truth.

When Bram is done eating and asleep again, I take

advantage of the early hour to take a long, hot shower before the gang gets up.

I put Bram in his crib with a move I've perfected to slide him on the mattress and drop his head gently so he won't wake up, and get naked. The warm water soothes my oversexed muscles—doing it in every corner of the house is not always comfortable and some positions require a certain athletic stamina—until my legs turn to jelly and the heat and the steam become too much and I have to get out.

I wrap myself in a towel and lay on the bed, extending my hand to Sam's side, regretful this won't be one of *those* mornings. Then, a minute before the alarm clock goes off, I turn it off and get dressed. I switch on Bram's monitor and go downstairs to make breakfast. Once everything is ready, I wake my princess with a series of tiny kisses Jo claims to hate and to be too grown-up to receive, but that I suspect she secretly loves.

"Mom," she shoves me away, indignant. "I'm awake, you can stop that now."

I sneak in one last kiss on her forehead before getting up. "All right, sweetie, time to get dressed, chop, chop."

Jo is very independent, so I leave her to choose her own clothes and move on to Will's room.

With him being younger, I'm allowed way more cuddles. I sneak into his twin bed and lift him onto my chest, just enjoying his weight on my ribcage for a while. When he stirs, I encourage the awakening with more serial kisses and a little tickling. Will wakes up, already smiling. He was a little sulky when we first met, but he's progressed to become a joyful, lively kid who smiles all the time.

Will turns his chin up and kisses me multiple times on the cheeks in return. I hug him closer to my chest.

"Mom?"

"Yes?" I ask, preparing myself for his usual plea to skip school.

"Do I have to go to school today?"

"Yes."

"Why?"

"So that you can get an education and become even smarter than you already are."

"And why do I need an education?"

"To be free to do whatever you want in life."

"I want to be a race car pilot. Do I still need an education?"

"Yes."

"Why?"

"Because then you're going to be a smart pilot."

Over my dead body, I add in my head. The sole idea of Will inside a race car at whatever age makes an icy shiver run down my spine. I don't even know how I'll cope when he'll be sixteen and driving around in a *regular* car. I shudder the fear away. That milestone is thirteen years in the future. No need to worry about it now.

"Since you're going to be a famous pilot, do you want to wear your *Cars* sweater to school today?"

"Yeeeeeeeeesssss!" he screams, covering my face with even more kisses.

I help him get dressed, and we make our way downstairs together. While Jo eats her milk and cereal, I feed Will his favorite blueberry yogurt and then get started on my breakfast.

Will gets bored pretty soon and demands to come down from his highchair. I let him down, he plays for a minute by himself, and then asks to sit in my lap.

"Let me finish eating, and then I can pick you up."

He looks at me with big puss-in-boots eyes and brings his hands over his stomach. "My tummy hurts."

I know I shouldn't encourage the lying, but I can't help the smile that tugs at my lips.

"Your tummy hurts?"

Will nods.

"And would sitting on Mommy's lap help cure your pain?"

Will nods again with a cheeky, scarcely toothed smile. How can anyone resist? He's just too cute. I pick him up, enjoy a long hug as he wraps his arms around my neck, and then I turn him over to finish my oatmeal. The usual battle for possession of the spoon and domain over the bowl—me, to eat, him, to play—begins.

Since it's raining outside, I pack everyone in the minivan, check that I've taken Bram's bag, that Jo and Will both have their bags and snack packets, and we're off.

At Jo's school, I execute a perfect drop-off. I pull up in the right lane, stop for exactly the allotted number of seconds, and I'm back on my way without the school traffic patroller even having to raise an eyebrow at me, let alone pick up his whistle.

At Will's kindergarten, I have to park, since three-year-old kids can't be dropped off by the side of the road. The rain is still pelting down without mercy. I debate trying to juggle an umbrella and a toddler and decide against it. I unbuckle Will's car seat—he loves to climb to the front on its own—and pull both our rain-jacket hoods low on our foreheads, asking, "Ready for a run?"

Will laughs like crazy all the way from the parking lot to the school and only mildly protests when I leave him with his teacher.

"Hi, Caroline," another out-of-breath mom calls out. A fellow rain jogger, I bet. "What a day, uh? Isn't Sam doing the drop-off this week?"

"No, he started on a new project and he's back to work."

The mom, whose name I don't remember, sighs dreamily. "Am I too forward if I tell you all the moms here would give an eye to have a husband like him. Sam has been the talk of the group ever since school started after the holidays."

"Has he? Why?"

"For one, he was the only dad doing the drop-off. And he's always so kind to everyone and looked so competent and involved with Will. I bet he even changes diapers and reads bedtime stories…"

I blink. "Don't all fathers do that?"

The woman laughs now. "Oh, dear, no. Nope. No way. My John doesn't know what a Diaper Genie is." She pats my shoulder. "He's a keeper, that husband of yours."

I leave the perhaps over-eager mom with mixed feelings swirling in my chest. On one side, I'm proud because Sam really is the best. On the other hand, I feel like a fraud. I landed in this perfect life thanks to one cosmic misalignment, I didn't *choose* it. The real me is the stupid cow who let Sam go, *the idiot!*

I'm still nervous and figuratively kicking myself in the butt when I get to work. So when Pam approaches me with a face that promises a verbal onslaught, I have zero tolerance and raise a hand to stop her and answer all her yet-unasked questions, "March book club, we have to make a pick I know. We should do romance again, yesterday's meeting was so enthusiastic. Some ladies wanted to double down again and go for two books also next month, what do you say about something tragic a la Nicholas Sparks and a comedy to compensate, perhaps the new Christina Lauren?"

Pam nods and takes a breath, ready to talk. I prevent her again, speaking first, "I uninstalled and reinstalled our administrative software last night before closing. If it still freezes, I've had it, we're going to upgrade. I saw the delivery truck pass me on the way, so I guess the new releases have arrived?"

She nods again.

"Then we can split the stocking of the shelves and, yes, you can have fantasy and young adult as long as you do the thrillers, too." I pause for breath. "Was that all?" I conclude. "Did I forget anything?"

Pam's mouth gapes open for a moment, then she closes it in a tight-lipped smile. "Is your memory coming back?" she asks.

"Nope," I reply.

Pam's smile fades and she points at my head. "I'm sure your memories are in there somewhere."

As the first signs of a panic attack—cold sweats, dry mouth, tachycardia—creep on me, I try to keep a poker face, and mumble, "Sure," before getting away with an excuse. I lock myself in the employee bathroom and hyperventilate in front of the mirror as I've just realized I'll never remember my kids being born, or Jo's first word, or Will's first steps.

I splash water on my face, trying to remain calm. It's okay. It's already a miracle that I stole Jersey Caroline's life. For the millionth time, I wonder what I'm doing here, how it's even possible, but the only explanation I came up with is that in this parallel universe Jersey Caroline died hitting her head, and while we were both in a coma, we switched places.

Oh my gosh, does that mean I kicked the bucket in my

world? Oh, hell, if the future Melodie showed me is to be any reliable, no one will be too heartbroken. Except maybe my parents and my sister, who, inexplicably, still love me in the present.

As my breathing slowly returns to normal, I decide that if one Caroline really had to die, it's better that I went. Jersey Caroline, besides being a mother of three, is way happier than I ever remember being in my old life. Sure, she has to put up with a little more poop, regurgitation, baby food, and tantrums than ideal, but she is loved—I am loved. The kids love me, Sam loves me, and everyone I know likes me. I wouldn't go back now, I *could not* go back to that life.

Another deep breath and I'm ready to return outside. I drop my bag in the office and since Pam has already started with the stocking, I help a college kid locate *The Official LSAT Handbook* and check him out.

I'm changing the registry's paper roll when the bell over the entrance door chimes, signaling a customer has entered. I look up and my old life and new one collide.

Jackie Marley enters the shop. She gives the place a once-over, which ends in a meh expression—slight downturn of her lips and an eyebrow raise—as if she was expecting much more than what she's seeing. She shuffles about the two large, round tables at the entrance with our featured new releases, opens a hardback or two, and recloses them after a few pages, still deeply unimpressed.

When I can stand it any longer, I come out from behind the counter and go to greet my former partner—in this life just an ex-colleague I haven't seen in seven years.

"Jackie," I call out loud. "Is that really you?"

She spins on her five-hundred-dollar heels and gives *me* a once-over. Her smile widens, probably to compensate for what she's really thinking. "Caroline!" she exclaims, and while her lips keep smiling, her eyes roam over my clothes and widen slightly. Jackie looks as disgusted as I initially was when I first perused Jersey Caroline's closet. But nowadays, fancy clothes and designer labels have no appeal. All I care about is that the stuff I wear is comfy and machine washable *and* dryable. Plus, I get spilled on or painted on too often to wear anything remotely high fashion. And sweatpants also have the privilege of being easy to pull down in case Sam is around—no pesky zippers that get stuck, no hard buttons to wrestle open, just a cozy, yielding elastic band.

"You look fabulous," Jackie lies through her teeth. The moment her visit is over, she's probably rushing home to wash the suburban taint off herself. Which poses the question: what the hell is she doing in my shop? "You haven't changed a bit," she proclaims, as if it were a big compliment.

She, on the contrary, has had a little work done—nose, lips, boobs—nothing too obvious. The best plastic surgery money can buy.

"You look wonderful, too." And since I can't stand her presence much longer, I cut to the chase. "What brings you into this neck of the woods? Got lost?"

"Aww, Caroline, can't an old friend visit?" *Not when we haven't seen each other in seven years.* "You know I was heartbroken when you never came back to work after having Lo."

"Jo," I correct her, thinking she didn't even wait for my maternity leave to be over before she stole my idea of founding a new publishing company taking with her all of Bucknam's unsatisfied authors. Jackie left out the Wilkins part of the name and went for a clean Marley Press instead, executing my plan to the last detail—or so the internet told me.

"Ah, Josephine, right, I forgot about your *Little Women* obsession. Anyway, I don't know if you've heard about the independent press I'm running," she says with false modesty.

Finally, we're getting down to business. "Sure," I say, hoping flattery will help me get rid of her faster. "Everyone has heard of Marley Press."

"Really?" she asks, throwing another side-stare at the new release table. "Because you don't stock many of our titles."

Try *none* of them. "They're not for our target audience," I explain.

"Which would be?"

Amazing readers who want to lose themselves in a beautiful story. "Aw, you know," I say instead. "Small town folks."

"Even so, you held a release party for Isabel T. Mercer a few months ago that made quite a splash. Got a feature in the *New York Times,* everyone was obsessed with *We Raise Together* for weeks."

"Yeah, great story," I confirm.

"The thing is," Jackie continues. "We're releasing this new memoir in six months by Ashlyn Farnborough, *My First Twenty-five Years,* and we're sparing no expenses for the launch. It's going to be an instant bestseller."

"Yeah, it will," I say, blushing with shame. That crap book is the same I picked over Yashika's debut author. In my previous life, I was as blinded by greed and an easy buck as Jackie is in both worlds. In my role as CEO of Wilkins and Marley, I couldn't see we were publishing one trashy title after the other. Publications no one would remember in a few years, but guaranteed to fatten our coffers in the immediate.

"Congratulations," I add. "But I don't see what this has to do with me or the shop."

"The thing is that Ashlynn saw the big splash *We Rise Together* made and the fuss the media kicked up… and she's put it in her head she won't have her release party anywhere but here, you know how stubborn celebrities can be," she says with a tone that implies—*you have no idea at all, you simpleton suburban housewife with a hobby bookshop you run to avoid day-drinking.*

To be fair, that's exactly how I judged this alternative version of myself when I arrived in this universe.

"Sorry, Jackie, but Ashlyn Farnborough's first twenty-five years wouldn't be a good fit for our readers."

"Of course, we'd pay a pretty penny to host the party in your store," Jackie continues as if I haven't spoken at all.

I shake my head. "Still not a good fit, I'm sorry."

"Come on, I'm sure your *business* could use a little cash influx." Again, she says business as if she meant *silly pet project.*

"Thanks for your concern, but we're doing just fine."

That's my competitive nature kicking in. I know I should be the bigger person, but her invasion of my turf with her Prada coat, Manolo Blahnik, and general Manhattan snobbism, has rubbed me the wrong way. I'm perfectly aware I don't need to compete with this woman, on any level. Her life's goals dangle at the end of a Botox needle and how many zeroes her bank account can reach. All things I left behind me. Despite that, I feel the irresistible urge to defend my choices to her. "We're opening a second store in Boston in a few months."

"A *second* store?" she asks, faux-impressed. "You don't

say."

"Yep, the first of many more. In ten years, we could replace Borders."

"Well, let's hope you don't end up in the same ditch instead. Is your word final on the release party?"

"Yeah, celebrities' first twenty-five years of very interesting life are really not a target for my readers."

"A dollar left on the table is a dollar lost," she trills.

"I can live with that."

"Very well, I wish you all the best with your little shop and your small life."

Jackie storms out a la Cruella Devil, door slamming and glass rattling included.

I go behind the bar and make myself a latte I don't drink. I keep the warm paper cup between my hands and stare at the foam, reflecting.

In my universe, that is the woman I chose as my partner. The idea now makes me recoil. And while Jackie and I were never best friends even in my old life, Manhattan Caroline more than tolerated her. Gosh, I *was* Jackie. Two peas in a publishing house.

I'm glad I never have to go back to that life.

Seventeen

Yes

Jackie's visit keeps me distracted throughout the rest of the day. I don't have the right concentration to tackle any high-level task. But to keep my hands busy, I climb down a deep tidying rabbit hole where I scour the shelves for series and make sure the books are arranged in the correct order. I start with fantasy, then science fiction, young adult, and romance. Until Pam finds me in the cozy mystery aisle—probably the most serialized shelf in the shop and the one I should've sorted first—and asks, "Shouldn't you have left already to go pick up the kids, like, ten minutes ago?"

I stare at my watch and panic. "Oh my gosh, you're right."

I scramble to my feet and rush around the shop to collect all my belongings: my bag, Bram's bag, coat, car keys… Just as I'm heading for the door, Pam calls after me, "Aren't you forgetting something?"

I stare at her with an interrogative expression, and she turns her gaze toward the office.

"Was I supposed to do something before I left, do I have to sign an order?"

"No," Pam says. "The baby, you're forgetting the baby."

"Bram!"

Thankfully, I've put him to sleep directly in his car seat, anticipating he'd still be sleeping when I had to leave. I grab the plastic handle of the seat and, loaded like a mule, I trudge toward the car. At least it's stopped raining and there's no traffic in our small town, so I arrive at Will and Jo's schools on time. In the car, on the way home, Jo is awfully quiet.

I check on her repeatedly in the rearview mirror, but her expression stubbornly remains the same: slight pout, arms crossed over her chest, gaze lost out the window.

"Jo, is something the matter? Bad day at school?"

Our eyes meet in the mirror. "No, I'm fine."

"You seem a little... um... preoccupied."

"Of course, I'm preoccupied, Mom. Mrs. Silvermore screwed up my plans for the Art Fair."

"First off, language, young lady," I say. And never in a million years would I've thought such a phrase could exit my mouth. I'm such a mom. "And how come she *ruined* your idea?"

"I had this entire fairy tale theme planned in my head. I wanted to build an enchanted forest with a white horse and Prince Charming and Snow White and the dwarfs and all the animals... it would've been wonderful."

"And why can't you make it?"

"Because Mrs. Silvermore decided this year, we're not going to have a simple art fair, but a *science*-art fair, and we must incorporate something scientific in our projects. And let me tell you, Mom, there's nothing scientific about fairy tales. Is there?"

"I can't think of anything off the top of my head, but I'm sure we can find something artistic, fairy-tale related, that is also scientific."

"Can we, Mom, really?"

We'd better.

At home, the house smells delicious, and I almost collapse with relief when I find Sam behind the stove intent on making dinner. The kids—those who already walk—rush toward him and each grab one of his legs, screaming,

"Daddy!"

I'm much slower with Bram in my arms and the two million bags I had to get off the car, but I soon catch up and hug him, too. He looks adorable with a silly "stand back, Dad is cooking" apron.

Sam gives me a long kiss and then kisses the top of Bram's head.

"Smells delicious," I say. "What are you making?"

"Tacos."

My stomach growls in anticipation. "Come on, kids, let go of Daddy's legs so he can finish making tacos."

They reluctantly do, but before we go upstairs for baths and to change, Will stares up at Sam. "I missed you at breakfast today, Dad."

Sam ruffles his hair and squats down to pick Will up. "And I missed you, too. But I had a sudden inspiration, and I had to go to the studio to sketch."

"And how did it go?" I ask.

"Oh, Charlie Bear, it was unbelievable. I drew all day. I didn't even stop for lunch and I had to quit only because my hands were cramping too bad." His eyes lit up. "The new spa will be amazing. I have this whole River Gods garden design in mind. It's going to be my best work to date."

"You say that every time."

"It's what we artists have to tell ourselves to keep going, that our next project will be our best." Sam drops Will to the floor and grabs a wooden spoon to stir the vegetables.

"What about you, Charlie Bear, how was your day?"

"Eh," I say. "Different."

One last stir and Sam turns to give me undivided attention. "Good different or bad different?"

"Weird different. Jackie came to visit me."

"Jackie? Do we know any Jackies?"

"*Marley?*" I specify.

Sam frowns. "What did she want?"

I tell him about the release party and my refusal.

"Did she get nasty when you said no?" Sam asks. "I never liked that gal."

"Not too openly, but she treated me with contempt like I was a nobody and she acted like this big-shot business woman."

Sam hugs me, pressing my head to his hard chest. "That woman might have all the millions in the world, Charlie Bear." Sam cups my face and lifts my chin up to force me to look at him. "But what does it matter when she has no soul, no heart, no passion?" My heart beats faster because I can't help thinking that's what Sam would think of me if he met the real me, or more the *old* me. "That woman isn't worth your pinky toe," he concludes.

I bury my face into Sam's neck, as I can't stand the love and admiration I see in his warm eyes. My soul used to be as dark as Jackie's, and I'm living this amazing life only because a much better version of myself died in a freak accident leaving behind three orphans. Then the universe decided they didn't deserve to grow up without a mother or for Sam to become a widower at such a young age, and so the Christmas spirits scanned all the parallel dimensions for a worthless version of Caroline that no one would miss too much—or at all—and they picked *me!* Well, Universe, thank you. I got a second chance and I'm not about to waste it.

I kiss Sam one last time and ask Jo and Will to please follow me upstairs. After quick baths and outfit changes, we wait for dinner to be ready in the basement—aka the kids' playroom. First, I set Bram down on his play gym to roll and experiment with the dangling, stimulating bits. One kid sorted, I grab a handful of books from the shelves and ask Will to build me a bridge—he gets to work immediately. And finally, keeping two heavy hardcovers for myself, I scoop Jo up and sit her on my lap, ignoring her protests that she's too grown-up for this.

"Do you want to help me find a scientific fairy tale or not?"

She quits trying to escape me and eyes the books in my hands. "What are these?"

"The original fairy tales," I say. "Hans Christian Andersen and the Grimm brothers, if we can't find something here, then we're screwed."

"Language, old lady," Jo reprimands me.

I tickle her in response. "Who did you call an old lady?"

Giggles over, I open the first book, shuffle a few pages, and stop on the tale of *Little Red Riding Hood.*

"How about this one?" I ask Jo. "If the wolf eats grandma, can we explore the wolves' digestive system?"

"Ew, Mom, that's like the worst idea ever."

I kiss her temple. "Perhaps you're right. Let's see if we can find something a little more romantic."

By the time dinner is ready, Jo and I have settled on creating an ocean project with mermaids with a scientific explanation of how sea-foam forms. Decomposed algae aren't much more romantic than wolves' digestive apparatus, but at least we'll have pretty fish and mermaids. In the time it took us to settle on this project, Will has built a spectacular bridge with six widthways, and Bram has rolled left, right, blabbed nonsense, and worked on developing his motor skills.

The tacos taste as good as they smell, and Sam even offers

to do the dishes and watch over a sleeping Bram while I put the older kids to bed.

Two bedtime stories later, I stroll the upstairs hall picking up the kids' shoes, stray clothes, the cat toys, half-full cups of nighttime water, miscellaneous school supplies, and other random rubble. Then, I change the cat litter, pack up Jo and Will's backpacks, and don't have the energy left to even watch TV on the couch with Sam. I'd fall asleep within ten minutes and then resent having to walk back up the stairs to go to bed. I brush my teeth and when I can't find my phone charger, I don't bother to go search for it downstairs, I simply open Sam's nightstand drawer to steal his—and find my Christmas present for him instead: the engraved stone.

I put on a heavy robe and walk out onto the balcony, cradling the stone in my hands, thinking.

When I'm ready to get back into the bedroom, I find Sam already tucked in bed. The hubby is reading a book—one of his high fantasy tomes that he still refuses to read in electronic format. Why? I mean the weight alone. But he claims he needs to feel the weight of the book in his hands and the grain of the paper under his fingertips.

"All that creativeness got yah, uh?" I say, upon seeing him in bed before nine. I drop the stone on the chest of drawers and get rid of the robe to steal Sam's white T-shirt from the chair where he's left it. The cotton is warm but smells too soapy for him to have worn it all day.

I give another, more theatrical sniff, asking, "What's this? And where's your real T-shirt?"

He drops the tome and looks up at me, laughing at being caught. "The one I wore at the studio had to go, but that one cooked dinner with me."

I pull the T-shirt on and bring the stone to bed, scooting

under the covers with him.

"Are you too tired to talk?" I ask.

Sam sets the book on the nightstand and turns to me. "Should I worry?"

"No," I say. "It's going to be a good talk."

He smiles. "Then fire."

Without speaking, I give him the stone.

His eyes go wide. "What's this?"

"It's a yes," I say. "Written in stone."

"You mean you—?"

I nod. "I want to know what it's like to be pregnant, to feel the baby's first kick. As crazy as it sounds, I also want to experience childbirth and what it's like to hold a baby in my arms for the first time... Sam, I want to have another baby."

Sam is so choked up, he looks like he's about to cry.

"Now, now, don't get all soppy or I'll have to tickle you."

He closes the distance between us and pulls me into a bear hug. Tight, intense, and filled with love.

The hugging turns from pure to not-so-innocent. Sam's hands slide down my thighs, then he grabs me by the hips and scoots me closer still. "I know it's too soon, but I should keep my baby-making skills in perfect form for when the time comes to really try."

I smile. "Mmm, you're right, we wouldn't want you out of practice." And no matter that I was bone-tired half an hour ago, when Sam looks at me the way he is now, he could resuscitate me from the dead.

His fingers have already found the elastic band of my underwear when the bedroom door opens and Will walks in, rubbing sleep from his eyes.

"We have a visitor," I whisper in Sam's ear, and his hands

quickly return above the covers.

"What's up, sweetie?" I ask Will.

"Mom, I just remembered I forgot to give you a good night kiss," Will says, coming toward the bed.

"Are you sure?" I ask while he scoots into my arms. "Because I remember you gave me one just before your bedtime story."

Will shakes his head. "No, I didn't."

I caress the hair away from his forehead. "This isn't about you having a bad dream about a fish with legs waiting for you in the dark and wanting to sleep in the big bed with us?"

Since he saw a commercial on the Chinese New Year's parade where the traditional dragon—the fish with legs— was sauntering down the street, he's been having nightmares.

Will wraps his arms around my neck and hides his face in my hair. "Can I sleep with you, Mommy?" he whispers.

I look up at Sam, who gives me a *"Your call,"* eyebrow raise with a little side note of *"but you know if you say yes tonight, he's going to want to sleep with us for the next two years."*

Sam has a point, but I don't care. My child is scared of the dark, no way I'm sending him back to his room to sleep alone.

"Of course, you can stay," I say, hugging him closer to my chest.

Sam shakes his head benevolently and gives me a kiss on the forehead. "I love you. And I love you, too, little guy."

***

As predicted, Will ends up sleeping with us for the rest of the week. And while sleeping with Will in my arms has been a treat for me, he can't go on being afraid of the dark.

Sam and I came up with a plan to cure his fear that we set in motion over breakfast on Saturday.

Sam is at the stove flipping pancakes he then piles on a plate. I tried to make those once, but my first attempt was bad enough for me to give up ever trying again. I suppress a smile as I remember the morning I put the batter in the blender because it looked like the closest thing we had in the kitchen to a mixer and it exploded on me, splattering half the batter on myself, the walls, the cat, and all three miniature humans. The other half of the batter, I miserably burnt. The kids ended up sticky and dirty and with no food. I had to bring them to I-Hop as a consolation. After that experience, everyone agreed I shouldn't make pancakes from scratch ever again. Plus, my husband looks so hot as he flips the spatula with the same flare of a professional chef, it'd be a crime not to make him cook even if the final product wasn't as delicious as his pancakes are going to be.

Sam throws the last one on the pile and sits at the kitchen island with us, doling out pancakes and maple syrup.

Once everyone has had a bite, Sam gives me a curt nod, which I return, and turns to Will. "Little man, what do you say we take a trip just us boys, spend a little father-son time together?"

Jo replies before Will has even had time to understand what he's been asked. "That's so misogynistic, Dad."

Sam boggles his eyes at me as if to ask if that's standard vocabulary for a seven-year-old. I shrug and lean in to whisper in Jo's ear the real reason her dad has to go on a solo trip with Will.

Jo rolls her eyes, whispering back, "He's such a baby. I've never been afraid of the dark, not even when I was his age."

My heart pangs a little as I don't know whether her affirmation is true. Once again, I mourn the fact I'll never experience Jo's toddler years. How tiny she must've felt in my arms when she was a newborn, or how sweet her kisses must've been when she wasn't grown-up enough to measure them out. Then I consider the alternative I narrowly escaped—a life where Jo, Will, and Bram don't exist and where I haven't seen Sam in seven years—and my heart beats even faster. Part dread, part anxiety, mostly relief. And finally, my heart expands with joy, remembering the decision to try for another baby Sam and I made last night. I have nothing to complain about, I should count my blessings.

While I've been busy having a mini freak-out, Sam has convinced Will to go with him to the Chinese New Year celebration in the city. The plan is to make Will see that the fish with legs is actually a dragon costume with a bunch of people walking underneath it and thus exorcise his fear.

I cut another bite of pancake, twirl it in the syrup puddle on my plate until it's soaked, and put the sugar bomb in my mouth. Gosh, it's perfect. Fluffy, not soggy. Sweet, but not overly so. Pancake perfection.

I close my eyes and moan. Sam, who's probably as eager for a little intimacy as I am after a week with Will in our bed, grins at me and gives me a little wink that promises tonight, once Will is back in his room, he's going to let me see fireworks brighter than whatever the Chinese are planning downtown.

And if I had to capture happiness in a moment, this would be it. A simple family breakfast with my husband and my kids and the promise of endless more breakfasts just like this one. I, Caroline Wilkins, am incontrovertibly, disgustingly happy.

Eighteen

Firsts and Lasts

Will is so excited about the special boys' trip that the instant breakfast is cleared, he rushes to his room to get dressed on his own and then starts pestering his father until Sam agrees to leave.

They change into their coats and Sam picks Will up to come to say goodbye.

"We'll go for a smoothie or something," Sam says, kissing my forehead. "The parade won't start for another two hours."

"Have fun," I say, ruffling Will's hair. "Both of you." I kiss my boy's soft cheeks once, twice, and again, and again, until he starts giggling. Then I lift my chin and look at Sam.

The phrase "I love you so much" pops into my head, but for whatever reason, I don't say it and just kiss Sam on the lips. And then they're gone.

The moment the door closes, Jo hops down the stairs in her ballet gear, white tights, blush body, and hair up in a chignon. Only the boots on her feet are at odds with this ballerina persona, but she'll exchange them for pointes at the dance studio.

This Saturday it is Fan's turn to drive the girls to practice. Jo goes to the same ballet academy as Harper and Nora. Visibly in a hurry, my daughter puts her coat on and slings her gym bag over one shoulder just as the baby monitor comes to life with Bram's screaming as he awakens.

In the split second I glance up the stairs toward my crying

child, my other kid mumbles, "Mom, I'll go to Auntie Fan on my own, or we'll be late, see you later."

Jo exits, and the front door shuts before I've had a chance to say goodbye. I want to run after her, but Bram's crying is growing more frantic, so I give up on the goodbyes and rush to soothe the baby.

In the nursery, I pick Bram up and hug him close to my chest. "It's okay, mothersucker, Mommy is here."

I change his diaper and we sit on the floor to play with rattles and other grabbing toys, balls, his activity gyms, and board books. Once we run out of toys, I play peekaboo with him, and after the umpteenth repeat, Bram stretches his arms to be picked up. I lift him and sit with him on the nursing chair.

"Are you hungry?"

Bram answers with a gurgle and lifts his tiny hands to grab my chin, laughing.

Then he looks directly at me and, clear as day, he says, "Mommy."

My heart bursts in my chest as a shock wave of warmth spreads from my core up to the tips of my hair and down to the points of my toes.

"Did you just call me mommy, you clever, clever boy?" I ask, while tears well in my eyes.

"Mommy," Bram repeats, proud.

I hug him closer to my chest.

Bram burrows in my shirt in response, searching for my nipple. I give him a quick feed, and he soon falls asleep as we rock in the chair.

I stand up and drop him in his crib. I'm watching him sleeping peacefully when a loud bang resounds from outside. Then another, and another. The sound of a heavy ball striking metal.

Rage surges in my chest at whoever is being so inconsiderate of my sleeping baby. But dread soon replaces the fury as I remember the other time I heard that sound. It was the last time I saw Melodie.

Is she back?

Bang!

Why?

Bang!

What does she want?

Bang!

I sit on the rocking chair and rock back and forward, nibbling at my cuticles and trying to ignore the noise. But it—*bang, bang, bang*—drills a hole in my skull worse than the Chinese drop torture.

When I can't stand it any longer, I grab Bram's monitor and head down the stairs, banging the front door open without even putting on a coat.

I run to the end of the patio and yell, "What do you want?" over the hedge separating my house from that of the neighbors'.

Melodie, her luminescent white-blonde hair lifted in matching pigtails, stops the basketball in her hands and looks up.

"Ah, Caroline, nice to see you, too. And to answer your question, I've come to take you home."

"I am home," I say.

Melodie snickers. "What? This dump in a New Jersey suburb? This isn't your home. You're Caroline Wilkins, you live in a swanky penthouse in Manhattan. Or have you forgotten who you are?"

"I'm not that person anymore."

Melodie smiles a cryptical smile. "Good, good," she says, bouncing the ball on the concrete. "Then my job here is done. Time to go."

Panic swells in my chest. "I can't go with you, I won't."

"Not how it works, Caroline, I told you this was only temporary."

"But then you disappeared, you left me here for weeks, you made me believe this was—"

"Forever?" she interrupts me, shrugging. "Sorry if I gave you the wrong impression."

I stomp my foot on the patio while half-freezing to death in my light sweatshirt and yoga pants. "I won't go," I repeat as I think of Will laughing as I kissed him on his puffy cheeks, or that I didn't tell Sam "I love you" one last time, or even said goodbye to Jo, and Bram, I won't leave him alone and helpless in his crib to wake up without a mother.

I'm about to run back into the house and shut myself in, when from across the yard, Melodie yells, "Caroline, catch!" and throws the basketball at me.

By reflex, my hands shoot up to grab the ball, letting go of the white baby monitor I'm holding. The last thing I see is the plastic rectangle falling on the patio's boards and splintering into a million pieces. Then the world spins and disappears in a white and gray vortex.

Nineteen

Back to the Real World

I blink awake in a panic, staring at a ceiling I don't recognize. A young girl's voice screeches next to me, "Mom, she's awake."

Tiny arms wrap around my neck, and on instinct, I hug my daughter to my chest and smell Jo's hair. Only the scent is wrong. I pull back and find Harper's hazel eyes staring back at me instead of Jo's blue ones.

I peek over her shoulder, where my entire family is holding their breath—Mom, Dad, Fan, Elijah, and their other three kids perched around the room like little monkeys. My eyes keep searching the space for Sam and Will and Jo, and who's taking care of Bram while I'm here?

Wait, where am I?

I must've asked this last part aloud because my mother replies, "The hospital, honey, you fell last night and hit your head, remember?"

I stare at my dad, looking for confirmation. "Merry Christmas," he says. "You gave us a fright."

"Christmas?" I ask. "Christmas was two months ago."

The adults blink at me and then exchange weirded-out side glances.

"Where's Sam?" I ask no one in particular.

"S-Sam?" My dad stutters back.

My mom looks at me, aghast. "You mean Sam," loaded pause, "Crawley?"

"Of course. Who else? Is he looking after the kids? Is that

why he isn't here?"

"Whose kids?" Fan asks.

"Mine," I reply indignantly.

At which Fan bursts out laughing.

"What's so funny?" I ask.

"Sorry," she replies between chuckles. "It's just that the idea of you with kids is so... so..." she can't even finish because she laughs again.

Tears well in my eyes and I stare at my mom. "Mom, where is Sam?"

Mom, looking sympathetic, wrings her fingers together as she replies. "Sweetie, you broke up with him—what was it now? Six? Seven years ago?"

"And we never got married?" I ask, my lower lip wobbling.

Mom shakes her head, dismayed.

"And I don't have kids?"

Fan stops laughing. "Are you being serious? You pity people with children!"

The reality that I've come back to my barren, childless, Sam-less universe hits me in the chest all at once and I start sobbing uncontrollably.

At this point, my family freaks out for good and while Elijah ushers the kids away from the crazy aunt, Dad goes searching for a doctor, while my mother and my sister sit on either side of my bed trying to console me.

I'm inconsolable.

A nurse has to come in and give me a mild sedative while a doctor explains to my family that a state of confusion is perfectly normal after a head trauma and a night spent in a pharmacological coma.

Ah, I retort in my mind, *try spending two months in an*

alternative universe, and then you talk to me about confusion, Doc.

After a while, I get the sobs under control. The sedative has forced my heart to stop beating so hard and fast it felt as if it was trying to escape my ribcage to go jump out the window and drown its sorrow into the Hudson. Poor heart, can I blame it for wanting out? In the past two months, it has received more love and joy than in the past seven years of my life combined.

I have to push the thought away to stop another panic attack from coming.

Once I'm calm enough to speak, I study my family, now warily reassembled into the room, and ask, "Why aren't you home celebrating?"

Mom steps forward. "The doctor said they'd wake you today, and we didn't want you to spend Christmas alone in a hospital ward."

That's the final straw. The tremble in my lower lips returns, and I turn into a sobbing mess again—only this time it's for gratitude instead of loss.

My relatives stay with me all day, and the nurses close an eye on the violated visiting hours with it being Christmas and all. But as the sun sets outside, not even the kinder nurse can pretend it's normal to have five adults and four kids crammed into a tiny room and my family has to go.

Mom offers to stay with me. I'm tempted to accept before I notice the dark circles under her eyes and remember she's already spent last night with me, reading *Little Women.* Such a long time ago to me, but for her, it's only been half a day. I send her home and once I'm alone, I quietly cry myself to sleep thinking how I'll never be able to read Jo or Will another bedtime story. Or tell Sam that Bram spoke his first word, or say I love you to any of them.

***

A weight shifting on my feet wakes me up. For a moment I think it's Mr. Winkle-Whiskers who has come to sleep on our bed and I push up on an elbow, elated, deciding the hospital scene has only been a bad dream. But when I blink twice to shake away the sleep haze, my eyes focus on the person at the foot of the bed and narrow.

"You," I hiss, and sit upright.

The movement is too sudden and makes me so dizzy I have to sink back on the pillows.

"Careful, Caroline," Melodie mocks me from the other end of the bed. She's back to wearing her white tunic, and her annoying hair is up in a ponytail. "You've hit your head pretty hard, you should take it slow."

"Go away," I say, crossing my arms over my chest and turning my face to the side.

"Oh, tsk, tsk, is this the way to greet an old friend?"

"Friend? We're no friends... Before I met you, I was perfectly happy and now I'm miserable. Thank you very much for nothing."

Melodie arches an eyebrow at me. "Were you... happy?"

Whatever I was about to retort dies on my lips and I have to close and open my mouth before I admit, "Okay, no. I wasn't happy. But I had no idea how unhappy I was, which made me at least... I mean, at least I could function, and now, now..." the wobble comes back and I let out an inhuman scream before I start crying again.

"Good, good," Melodie says. "Let the beast loose, it's therapeutic."

"Therapeutic? Are you delusional? All that crap about it's

better to have loved and have lost than never to have loved is bullshit," I say. "Blissful ignorance is my jam. But thanks to you I've never felt worse in my entire life."

"And what are you planning to do about it?"

"What do you mean? What *can I* do?"

"Anything… everything?"

"How?"

Melodie hops off the bed and stands behind it, placing her hands on the horizontal foot bar. "You're not dead, are you? And your stubborn, albeit slow-to-catch-up brain has taken a hit but is still working, right? I'm sure you'll find a way."

"To do what?"

A bell chimes in the distance, and Melodie floats off the floor and drifts toward the window. "To turn your life around, Caroline, I thought it'd be clear by now that was the whole point." Her contours are becoming more luminescent and less defined by the second. But I can still make out her eyes as she winks at me. "Merry Christmas," she says, and then disappears in a flash of bright white light just as the bell outside rings its twelfth stroke.

Twenty

Going Back Home

By the time I'm dismissed from the hospital the next morning, I've already called my chauffeur and arranged an emergency meeting at the offices of Wilkins and Marley for this afternoon. But before that, I ask Nelson to drop me off at home to shower and to please wait for me outside.

As I step into my pristine apartment, the excess tidiness makes my blood freeze in my veins. This is a cold-hearted house inhabited by a cold-hearted woman. I unzip my red boots and kick them off, leaving them strewn between the entrance and the living room to create at least a little chaos.

After the shower, I step into my closet, but without the usual pang of satisfaction I felt every time I got to admire the tangible proof of my worldly success. Dear expensive clothes, how little you mean to me now.

The walk-in closet is riddled with dresses, but I haven't worn a pencil skirt in two months and I'm not in the mood to start again today.

I have to scroll to the very back to find a pair of jeans and a simple cashmere sweater. The lowest-heeled shoes I own are a pair of beige suede ankle boots so I go for those.

If my driver is surprised to see my "casual" attire—still ten times fancier than everything I wore in my mommy days—he doesn't say.

Nelson opens the car door for me and then gets in on the other side. Once he's in the driver seat, gloved hands on the wheel, he asks, "Where to, Miss?"

"Home," I say dramatically.

Then, as Nelson shoots me a perplexed stare in the rearview mirror since we're parked right outside my building, I explain, "My parents' house."

Before we reach my childhood neighborhood, I ask Nelson to make a deviation to Russel Square.

He takes a lap of the roundabout until I ask him to stop in front of the old pharmacy. In this world, the building is abandoned and forlorn. No one has restored the crumbling establishment and instead of the pulsing heart of the square, it now looks like a gaping hole in its chest. The windows are paneled with newspapers, except for the lower-left corner where the glass is broken and the paper has been torn by the wind. On the door, a "for sale" sign with a phone number underneath is almost too discolored to read. I point the camera of my phone at it and zoom in as I snap a picture. The image isn't super clear, but the number is readable. I send the photo to my attorney with the address and a few lines of instructions to buy me the entire building.

Next, on to my parents' house. I'm not sure what I expect as I ask Nelson to pull up a few houses before my actual parents' house in front of the house Sam and I lived in my dream. I'm calling it a dream because it's shorter than out-of-body-parallel-universe sabbatical.

The house is up for sale as well and uninhabited from the looks of it.

Was I expecting a different family to sleep, laugh, and grow together inside those four walls? And would that have been better than seeing the building unloved and crumbling down, same as the bookshop? A white-picked foreclosure sign is planted in the lawn out front with the name of a real estate agent on it.

I don't take a picture or ask my lawyer to buy it. The bookshop is for me... a new house? What use would it be without Sam?

The street is empty and eerily quiet. No one has seen me and I could simply ask Nelson to turn around and bring me back to Manhattan. That's what the old me would've done. But I'm not that Caroline anymore, am I?

Instead, I tell Nelson to park and walk up my parents' driveway.

When Mom comes to open the door after I ring the bell, she's utterly flabbergasted at finding me on her doorstep.

"Caroline," she says. "Are you okay? I called the hospital this morning to ask what time we should come to pick you up, but they told us you'd already left. I didn't think we'd see you until Easter."

That last jab hurts a little. I mean, not that my mom is wrong. Manhattan Caroline, they probably wouldn't have seen her until Easter, and if I found a good excuse, probably not until Thanksgiving.

I smile awkwardly. "Well, surprise," I say. "I hope you don't mind adding another plate to the table."

"Lunch won't be ready for another hour, but if you're okay waiting?"

"I have to be back in the city for a meeting this afternoon, but I'd like to stay if you'll have me. Actually..." I stare back at Nelson in the car, ready to freeze his ass off while he patiently waits for me for the next three hours, and my heart tugs. "How about *two* more plates?"

Mom smiles. "The more the merrier, we have a whole Christmas meal cooked that we didn't eat yesterday..."

"I'll be right in." I turn on my heels and hop back down the front steps to go knock on Nelson's window.

He rolls the glass down. "Yes, Miss?"

"Nelson, would you like to join my family for lunch?"

Nelson's jaw positively drops. "Miss, I—I couldn't."

A lot of convincing on my side, and stuttered, awkward replies on his later, I finally manage to drag Nelson out of the car and bring him inside.

He's a novelty to my sister's kids and so the older ones all focus on him for a second, pestering him with questions. Is he a pilot? Sort of. Can he also drive planes? No. How old is he? Fifty-four. Is he married? Yes, to Judith, has been for the past twenty-six years. Does he have any kids? Three grown children and two grandkids.

I note, not without shame, how I didn't know many of the answers to those personal questions. The thought of asking him has never even crossed my mind before. Gosh, what an asshole I used to be.

While Benjamin tries to convince Nelson to let him drive his car, I locate Fan and steal baby Tommy from her arms.

Fan is so surprised by my cheery approach that she doesn't realize I've relieved her of the baby until she sees me bouncing him on my hip.

"Caroline," she says, extending her arms as if to ask for the baby back. "Are you sure you want to hold him? Last time you ended up in the hospital."

"That was the ice, not the baby."

"What if he poops?"

"Then I'll change his diaper. A little poop never killed anyone."

"You don't change diapers!"

I smile at her. "Want to bet which one of us can do it faster?"

She's too shocked to protest further and lets me have her

baby.

I zig-zig through the various toys scattered on the living room floor and sit on the couch with Tommy.

I'm busy rocking him in my arms when Nora climbs on next to us.

"Auntie Caroline, how's your head? Does it hurt?"

I touch the bump in the back of my skull. "No, not too much."

Definitely not as much as my heart, I add silently.

"I'm glad you're okay."

This is the longest conversation I had to date with Nora. She looks at me a little intimidated, so I smile encouragingly.

"Is it true you work with books?" She promptly responds to my openness.

"Hm-mm. Do you like to read?"

Nora's eyes light up. "Oh, it's my favorite. Would you— would you—?" She starts and stops as if she didn't dare ask whatever it is she wants to say. Guess she isn't used to me paying her much attention the three times a year I visit. Gosh, I've been the worst aunt in the world. But that ends today. My nieces and nephews might be the only kids I'll ever get to love and spoil.

"What is it, sweetie? You can ask me anything."

"Would you read me a story, Auntie Caroline?"

"Which one?" I ask.

"*Sleeping Beauty,* but you have to make different voices for each character."

"Bring me the book and we'll see how dusty my acting skills are."

That's how ten minutes after I've entered my parents' house, I end up sitting on the large rug with baby Tommy in my lap and a circle of three attentive kids listening to me as

I do my best impression of Maleficent.

Elijah arrives about fifteen minutes before lunch is ready and even if I don't see him, I hear his shocked voice as he asks Fan, "Is that your sister reading to the kids?"

I double concentrate not to mess up my lines while still listening to how Fan replies.

"I have to google 'personality changes after head trauma' I wouldn't know how else to explain this."

"The kids seem to love it."

There's a pause and I can practically see Fan shrug.

"As long as it lasts."

Okay, I deserve a little distrust. But the new Caroline is here to stay. You'll see, family.

Lunch is awkward at first. Mom expresses her distress by smiling too much and talking in a tone a few octaves above her usual range. Nelson is doing his best to appear inconspicuous, probably still unsure of his grounding. Fan and Elijah keep exchanging weirded-out side-glances when they think I won't notice. Only Dad and the kids are oblivious to the others' discomfort and are having a jolly good time.

As for me, I'm having a blast with my nieces and nephews. I grab two sliced carrots and fix them under my upper lip, turning to Benjamin, growling. "Beware of the carrot monster." Benjamin and baby Tommy collapse in a fit of laughter while Nora and Harper chuckle along in a more dignified, older-sisters way. "Eat all your vegetables, Benjamin, if you don't want to experience my wrath."

Benjamin shrieks and makes a show of polishing off his plate. I sigh inwardly, imagining how Will wouldn't have eaten his broccoli, carrot monster, or not. He had made plenty of progress on the eating front, but certain vegetables were still labeled enemy number one.

Mom's triple-layered chocolate cake doesn't need any encouragement to be devoured by either adults or children, and by the time the meal is over, it's with real regret that I announce, "Sorry guys, Nelson and I have to go."

The raucous protests that erupt from the kids are both heartwarming and heartbreaking.

Benjamin in particular grabs on to my leg, pleading for another story while he rubs his eyes clearly ready for his afternoon nap.

I pick him up and hug him close to my chest. "Next time I come. I promise."

I hand him over to my sister and she scolds me, probably thinking, don't make promises you won't keep.

"Auntie." Nora tugs on my sweater.

I squat down next to her. "Yes, sweetie."

"When can we come to visit you in the city?"

I do a mental review of my schedule. "Why don't I have Nelson pick you up the day after tomorrow, and we can spend the entire day together." I look up at Fan. "If your mom agrees."

Nora and Harper dance at Fan's feet, chanting, "Please, Mommy, please, can we go?"

Fan's gaze sears through me. "Caroline, are you sure you can take care of three kids for an entire day, on your own?"

I stand up. "I'm pretty confident," I say, thinking of the past two months that only existed in my head but that still feel so real.

"And you don't have to work? No important meetings to go to?" she asks in a threatening *"let my kids down and I'll kill you,"* voice.

"I'll clear my schedule," I say.

Fan nods in a way that says, *"You get the benefit of the doubt, but screw up and you're out."*

I nod back in a, *"I won't"* reassurance.

Fan sighs. "Okay, kids! You can go!"

Cheers erupt all around, and I mouth a "thank you" at Fan.

The promise of a day out on the town allows me to leave without further protests.

In the car, Nelson tries to claw back some boundaries as he asks, "Where to, Miss Wilkins?"

"The office," I say. "And, Nelson?"

"Yes?"

"I told you, it's Caroline."

Twenty-one

A New Way

The offices of Wilkins and Marley are closed today. But our building, which we share with a couple of law firms, an investment fund, and a headhunting company, is used to dealing with workaholics and their on-holiday emergencies, so it's open and staffed with basic security even during the holidays or at night in true New York fashion.

When I step inside, the security guard, Edward his plaque reads, doesn't appear at all surprised to see me. I'm a notorious holiday avoider and late nighter.

"Afternoon, Miss Wilkins," he greets me.

"Afternoon, Edward."

The guard's eyes widen at my response. I'm not sure if Manhattan Caroline ever even replied to his greetings. "How was Christmas, did you have a good time with your family?"

"Y-yes," he replies, astonished.

A few more basic questions on my part are all it takes for him to grab his wallet and show me pictures of his five grandkids.

"And what about you, Miss Wilkins?" he asks after I've admired and praised the beauty of each of his grandchildren. "Was your Christmas good?"

"Yes." I smile, feeling bittersweet. "These have been the best holidays of my life, and please call me Caroline, Ed, won't you?"

On the way to the elevator, I feel the guard's stunned stare on me even after I've gotten in and pushed the button to the top floor. I imagine Ed staring at the moving elevator for as long as the spacious lobby allows and shaking his head in wonder before he remembers he's supposed to be calling my secretaries to alert them I've arrived and promptly do so.

When the elevator doors ding open, Annabelle and Debra are waiting for me outside, looking a little out of breath. As if Edward's five-second delay forced them to run down the long office hall, which it probably did.

"Good afternoon, Miss Wilkins," Annabelle greets me.

"Good afternoon, ladies," I interrupt before she can recite all the work-related info I've trained her to give me the moment I step out of the elevator.

Once again, I ask both of them how Christmas went, make a little conversation, and request for them to call me Caroline from now on. They're even more stunned than Edward or Nelson. As my closest collaborators, they aren't used to any mollycoddling on my part.

Both assistants are still staring at me with that deer-caught-in-the-headlights expression when I prompt Annabelle to go on with the list of info I need.

By the time she replies, we're already standing in my office.

"Nothing much happened yesterday, the numbers for the last-minute holiday sales reports on *How to Décor Your House like a Celebrity* are extraordinary." She hands me a printout, and I try not to wince at the book title.

I don't even look at the numbers I would've pored over with greed once, and merely ask, "Anything else?"

Annabelle is too shocked by my attitude to reply, so Debra takes over. "Miss Marley has already arrived and is waiting for you in conference room Ophelia."

"What about Yashika?" I ask. "Is she coming?"

"I'm here." A panting Yashika appears on the threshold, leaning on it.

I raise an eyebrow. "Did you run all the way from home?"

"No, but I was visiting my parents in Maine and I only got your notification this morning so I had to rush back on two different trains and—"

"Oh my gosh, Yashika, I'm so sorry," I interrupt her and all three women gape at me. No one in this office has probably heard me apologize, like, ever. "I didn't know you were visiting your family or I wouldn't have called. Please, take next week off, and I'll pay for your ticket to go back north. Now, shall we? I'd like you all to be present for the meeting."

The women exchange side glances that range from wary to shocked to incredulous and follow me down the hall.

The Ophelia meeting room is our grandest with a long, rectangular table that can easily accommodate thirty people, glass walls at the front and back—windows technically—and a grand crystal chandelier dangling from the ceiling.

Ophelia is the room we use for all-staff meetings where the editors make their pitches for books they want to publish and anyone, from interns to secretaries, can bring forward an idea. At least it used to be like that in the early days. I don't remember the last meeting where a book wasn't pitched by a senior editor.

Ophelia is an odd choice, considering I've asked Jackie for a tête-à-tête.

My partner is waiting for me seated at the closest corner of the table—not the head—on the windows side with her back to the view.

Jackie is wearing a cream wool suit with a pencil skirt and a cape jacket that makes a stark contrast with her long bob of straight licorice-black hair. The company's lawyer, a thirty-something Persian Adonis, is sitting on her right. I more than suspect their relationship of not being strictly professional, but he has an uncanny eye to comb through overlong, tiny-written contracts and spot any potential traps, so I've never objected to Farhan's position.

Without hesitation, I pull the glass door open, and with a brisk, "Good afternoon," I position myself on Jackie's opposite side, facing the windows. The sun is already setting and its low glare above the horizon forces me to squint my eyes before they get adjusted. Did Jackie choose the positioning on purpose? Like an opponent army choosing its vantage point on the battlefield to blind the enemy. I also wonder when Jackie and I stopped being friends. I guess the more the company made money, the more we progressed from friends to business associates and finally partners who don't particularly dote on each other.

I consider making the effort of a few minutes of polite conversation before getting to the point, but Jackie Marley is the one person I can skip pleasantries with. She has always been a cut-to-the-chase kind of gal.

"Afternoon, Caroline," Jackie replies, taking in my casual clothes with predatory interest. And true to character, she promptly asks, "Do you mind telling us why you had to drag us to the office on one of the few days of the year we're closed? What was so important that couldn't wait until tomorrow?"

"I'm sorry, did I pry you from the arms of your loving family…?"

Jackie scoffs. "More saved me from their claws. I swear, if I have to listen to another Christmas carol I might start to wear ear wax plugs even during the day."

The old Manhattan Caroline would've agreed with her soundly. The new me, not so much.

"Good," I say. "And to answer your question, I've asked you here today because I thought we'd better be alone to discuss what I'm about to propose." I gesture at Farhan. "There was no need to bring the legal department into this, by the way."

"I don't know, Caroline, you call me out of the blue asking for an urgent meeting. I wasn't sure what to expect."

"Nothing sleazy, I assure you. On the contrary, you'll be pleased with what I'm about to propose. And, Farhan, sorry if we've interrupted your holiday."

Farhan mumbles a "not at all" before throwing a side glance at Jackie that makes me wonder if they were already together when I called.

I nod at him and continue, "Actually, it might be a good thing that you're here."

"Please, Caroline," Jackie interrupts, "the suspense is killing me."

"All right," I say. "I've decided to accept your offer."

"What offer?"

"The one to buy me out."

A collective gasp spreads across the room, and not even the usually impassible Jackie can hide her surprise.

Jackie recovers faster and narrows her eyes at me. "What's the catch?"

"No catch."

She leans back in her chair, pensive.

"I thought you'd be happy. You've been asking me to sell you my majority stake for ages."

"Yes, and you've always refused. What's changed?"

I tell her the truth. "I had a near-death experience which

made me reassess my priorities."

Jackie chuckles. "Oh, Caroline, please don't tell me you're going soft on me." Then her gaze turns shrewd. "And I know you too well, you're not planning to strip yourself of all your possessions and become a Good Samaritan. You have something in mind."

"Yes." No point in denying it. I want to make Rumpelstiltskin a reality, beginning with one store and then expanding. But I want my cake and to eat it too, as I plan to also be a publisher, but not for the rubbish we've been printing lately at Wilkins and Marley. "I'll branch out on my own. We can both agree our partnership has gone as far as it could."

Jackie leans her elbows on the table. "You won't be able to take any of our authors with you like we did when we left Bucknam."

I keep myself in check not to scoff. "Don't worry, I don't want them. But," I turn to the three women sitting on my left. "I'd like to take Yashika, Annabelle, and Debra with me."

Their already slacked jaws dangle a little lower.

Jackie regards them as if she was appraising a nasty bin of trash. "Oh, you can have them."

"Good," I say, standing up. "Make me an offer. Give me your best number and Farhan can draft an exit contract. Our personal lawyers can review it, and the whole business can be over before the end of the year."

Jackie stands up as well. "You'll have my offer by end of day tomorrow."

"Great," I say. "I won't take up any more of your precious time."

I exit the room, and my three minions scramble to their feet to keep up with me.

In my office, I ask Debra, the last one in, to close the door and invite all three women to sit before my desk. "Don't just stand there like fish dangling from the hook, take a seat."

They do.

"Today might've come as a shock to you, but, trust me, this will be a great opportunity for you all." I turn my gaze on my senior editor. "Yashika, you were right about the direction we'd been taking. Things will change at my new company. You'll have complete creative independence and the budget to sustain your choices... except for your first novel..." Yashika's face, which has been growing brighter the more I speak, crumbles. "I want you to track down Kendall Hick's agent and make sure that *The Yellow Window* is the first book we publish." Her smile brightens again. "I heard they had an option with an incredibly obtuse publishing house that let them walk, but we're not going to be that stupid, are we?" I give Yashika a little wink. "Offer them whatever you feel is right. With the sale of my shares of Wilkins and Marley, I'll have enough to cover it."

Yashika nods, and I turn to the other two. "As for you, I assume you both got a degree in English Literature and came to work for a publishing house to become editors eventually, am I correct?"

They both nod sheepishly.

"And the reason you're still stuck as my assistants is that you feared that if you quit and I took it the wrong way, I would've zeroed your opportunities to work at any other publishing house in the city."

This time, they don't nod, but they don't deny it either.

"Well, you're both promoted starting today. Annabelle, you're going to be an editor, and Debra, you'll be her junior. I only need you to help me set up our new gig, you'll have to hire and train your replacements and a few admins before you start with the actual editorial work. The startup period shouldn't take more than a month or two. And, Annabelle, you've been with me long enough to know how it works, so spread the word with literary agencies that you're open for submission and the manuscripts should flow in naturally."

"Are we going to focus on any genre in particular?" Annabelle asks.

"No, do whatever you want, as long as the story is good. I only have one veto."

All three look at me expectantly.

"No celebrity biographies, or celebrity tell-all, or celebrity accounts of their first twenty-five very meaningful first years on the planet."

That declaration earns me three bright, eager smiles.

"Oh," I add. "I also need you to track down a Pamela Sutton and an Elsie Garner and ask both of them to come in for an interview, and girls... don't take no for an answer."

***

My professional life took less than a day to sort. Tomorrow, I'll meet with my real estate agent to look at some locations for the new offices. I shocked her when I specifically asked to steer clear of Manhattan. We're going to spend the day trudging around Brooklyn, the city's pulsing heart of startups and innovation.

But now that I'm sitting alone on my creamy white couch in my too empty apartment, I can't escape the question that has been terrorizing me all day and I've avoided asking myself at all costs: is Sam single in this universe?

I place my laptop on a pillow on my legs and with a beating heart, I open Facebook and tap Sam Crawley into the search box.

Facebook is considered a social network for old people now, and I'm glad we're both old enough to have a profile and that we're still friends. In fact, my Sam pops up at the top of the results page. His profile picture is one of him in a tux at some event, probably an inauguration for one of his mosaics. Sam is so devastatingly handsome and I love him so much my fingers tremble on the mouse wheel as I scroll down the "about" section to find his relationship status.

He doesn't have one.

No news is good news, I chant to myself. But the discovery doesn't ease my accelerated heartbeat, and my stomach ties itself into knots.

Since he isn't spelling it out for me, I scroll his profile backward for any hint that he's seeing someone.

Sam's posts are mainly of artistic pictures of his creations, from the sketches to the final mosaics with all the phases in between detailed in "behind the scenes" reportages.

Desperate to find any clues on his private life, I rifle through the recurring posts of happy birthday wishes, but nothing stands out. And Sam himself barely ever appears on his profile. I find a photo of him on a biking trip. One of his ten-year high school reunion. A selfie of himself at Madison Square Garden at a Knicks game. And a picture of him kissing a woman on a tropical beach at sunset.

Twenty-two

Happy New Year

My heart stops and I have to make an effort to swallow. I stare at the date in the picture. It was taken three years ago and the woman is tagged as Sylvie Dassault. I click on her name with my heart in my throat and enlarge her profile picture. She's a gorgeous brunette with blue eyes and a warm smile. In the photo, she looks tired but happy as she sits in a hospital bed with a baby in her arms. I can't see the baby's face and can't gauge if he or she bears any resemblance to Sam.

Adrenaline must prevent me from fainting on the spot as I scroll to her relationship status.

Married.

It doesn't say to whom or since when.

As cold sweat clams my palms, my back, and my forehead, I browse through her—thankfully non-private—profile and collapse with relief when a shot of her appears standing next to a handsome man with salt and pepper hair as they cradle a newborn baby in their arms. The man is a regular on her profile with pictures of them on vacations, at restaurants, and wedding shots.

Oh, thank goodness.

My anxiety returns to bearable levels. And my heart quiets down even further as I delve further into her timeline and find a relationship status change: *Sylvie Dassault is no longer in a relationship with Sam Crawley.*

I keep scrolling back to the time they *were* a couple.

Sylvie is the kind of person who posts everything on Facebook and never deletes a thing. Her profile is a lot more forthcoming in the stalking of my ex. I'm treated to shot after shot of their two years together. Again, comprising vacations, dinners out, long, romantic walks, even a bed selfie that makes me gag. I keep going until I find the writing *Sylvie Dassault is in a relationship with Sam Crawley.* And then scroll further to when Sylvie's posts portrayed her partying around Manhattan with her girlfriends.

I go back to the pictures of her and Sam together, but they're so sickening I shut the laptop and throw it to the side. I chew on my fingertips. So far I've only proved Sam is no longer in a relationship with Sylvie. But what about the other hundreds of thousands of single women in Manhattan?

On my phone, I pull up his Instagram profile. The first photo is an invitation to the grand opening of the Koi Hotel on New Year's Eve.

An air pocket forms in my belly.

Well, Caroline, certain field-researches are better done in person.

***

The five-day countdown to New Year's Eve is the most nerve-wracking week of my life. The days pass alarmingly fast and unbearably slow in a mix of dread and anticipation.

I spend most of my time hustling to set up the new company. I interview Pam, who's currently working at the Caldwell Public Library, and bring her to the original Rumpelstiltskin shop—still an abandoned pharmacy in this world. We click immediately. Even in this universe, we're bookish soulmates. As I tell her all my ideas on how to make this the best bookshop ever, she finishes my sentences before

I can give her the full vision. Pam and I are on the same page about everything. I hire her on the spot to be the store manager. Elsie is next and she's just as onboard.

Tuesday, I take a break from work to show Harper, Nora, and Thomas around the city as I promised. The day with the kids is more intense and consuming than any workday could ever be and is over too quickly. By Thursday night, I've signed the agreement with Jackie to dissolve our partnership and leased a new hip office building in Dumbo. Staff has been hired and the Rumpelstiltskin logo trademarked.

But Friday, I reserve the day for myself. I get the best pampering money can buy and also shop for a new dress. The same evening gown Sam had gifted me for Christmas, but in a smaller size because, well, my boobs aren't bursting with milk and this body hasn't given birth to three kids—yet.

I already have the shoes to go with the dress and the Manolo are as much of a perfect fit as I'd imagined in my dream.

Feeling like Cinderella, I ride down in the elevator ready to go to the ball. I only hope my prince hasn't found another princess in the seven years I ignored him.

My doorman opens the lobby door for me, saying, "You're a vision tonight, Miss Wilkins."

I beam at him. "Thank you, Philip."

Nelson's reaction is about the same as he holds the car door open for me.

The compliments give me a much-needed boost of confidence. But twenty minutes later, when Nelson pulls up in front of the Koi Hotel and, after opening my door, waits for me to get out, I'm petrified. I can't move.

If Sam has a wife or a girlfriend, he will have brought her tonight. What if I walk in there and find him on the arm of a gorgeous woman? What if he looks at her the way he looked at me in my dream? I could die of heartbreak on the spot. Heartbroken syndrome is a real thing, I've researched it.

"Is everything all right, Caroline?" Nelson asks.

"Not sure," I say, finally getting out. "But I will find out soon. Wish me luck."

Nelson taps his hat at me. "You don't need it. No sane man could resist you tonight." My driver winks at me.

How he guessed my anxiety is about a man is a mystery, but I smile at him anyway and nod.

"Do you want me to wait for you?"

"No, Nelson, go home, celebrate with your family. I'll take a cab," I say, while really hoping I'll spend the night making love to Sam for the first time in seven years just as in my dream—minus the milk spillage.

As I walk into the foyer, I'm momentarily stunned by how different the space looks. In this universe, without Jo to sway him, Sam has chosen the jungle theme. I'm standing in a tropical garden where green is the dominant shade, interspersed with the occasional splotch of color given by flowers and tropical birds.

I wouldn't even be able to say which design looks better. They're both stunning. And I could spend all night gaping at Sam's genius on display, but my priority now is to observe without being seen. A passing server offers me a flute of champagne and I gladly accept—a little liquid courage never hurt anyone. The bubbly fizzes on my tongue in a delicious spark.

With the glass in my hands, I move into a shadowy corner of the room. I'm basically hiding behind a giant Swiss cheese plant, which much resembles the ones on the walls.

Screened by the wide leaves, I frantically scan the hall,

looking for a head that will pop above the others by a foot. It doesn't take long for me to locate Sam. Even if his back is turned to me, I'd recognize that nape everywhere. Same dark, curly hair, same broad shoulders, and same sweet ass. Upon seeing him, my brain overflows with a million overlying thoughts. Part of me is busy lusting after him, remembering how intense his gaze is on me while we make love, or how his hands feel on my skin when he touches me. Another part is self-loathing, yelling how stupid I've been for letting such a man slip through my fingers. My ovaries want to have even more of his babies. And my heart is about to explode from how much I love him.

What am I going to do if he's with someone else?

Sam is standing in a tight-knit group of people, women too, but he's not touching any of them nor seems affectionate toward anyone. In my dream, when we came here together, he wouldn't keep his hands off me, not even for a minute. He'd always have a hand on my lower back or an arm looped with mine.

I observe him for a long time. Sam smiles, shakes hands, hands out business cards, but they all seem like business-related interactions. No PDAs so far. Also, the surrounding crowd keeps shifting and I can't detect any constant presence except his.

Could he… could he really be alone? Single?

My heart soars with hopefulness while my stomach clenches in anxiety, because now I have to go talk to him, and what I have to say sure won't be easy.

I drop my empty glass on a table, inhale, and take the first bold step in his direction.

Twenty-three

The End of It

My next step is less audacious, and by the third, my resolve wavers. Halfway through, I chicken out completely and divert toward the restrooms.

Inside, I would splash my face with fresh water or better even fill the sink and plunge my head underwater. But that would spoil the professional makeup I spent an hour at a saloon having applied and also ruin my blowout. I settle for opening the tap and let the cold water flow over my wrists to cool down.

I stare in the mirror and whisper encouragements to myself, "Caroline, you can do this, now you're going to march outside wearing your heart on your sleeve and admit how stupid you've been for letting things end the way they have between you two. Then you'll beg Sam to take you back and put as many children in you as fast as he can. Easy peasy."

I close the tap and dry my hands on a paper towel, nodding at my reflection. Pep talk received.

I apply a fresh layer of lip gloss and exit the room. I'm fumbling to close the clasp of my clutch, which I stuffed with too many things, and I'm not looking where I'm going until I bump into someone coming out of the men's room.

"Oh, sorry, I wasn't—" I say, but then I look up and meet Sam's gorgeous brown eyes, which widen.

"Caroline?"

"Sam," I squawk. Then clear my throat, trying to achieve

a normal speaking tone, and I repeat, "Sam." Only now it comes out too low. But third time's the charm and I finally manage to speak in a level voice as I breathe, "Hi."

"Hi, I haven't seen you in..." he falters, because the natural segue would be *I haven't seen you in seven years, not since you refused to bear my children and I had to kick you to the curb.* "...in forever," he saves.

A flush creeps up my cheeks. Things worsen when his gaze roams the length of my body in a subtle once-over.

Under his scrutiny, I feel practically naked. I know he likes this dress, he picked it for me. And I also know how much he'd enjoy taking it off. The mental image makes my nipples go hard and since I'm not wearing a triple-padded nursing bra, I'm not sure if it's showing. But judging from the way Sam's gaze flicks lower for a second and his pupils dilate, *it is* showing.

Sam coughs, embarrassed. "Sorry," he says. "I've been staring. You're the last person I expected to see tonight."

Does he mean... *oh, downer, what the hell is my ex doing showing up on the most important night of my career?* Or did he mean... *I haven't stopped thinking about you for a minute of the past seven years and you've never looked more beautiful even in my wildest dreams.* Well, he must've stopped thinking about me in the two years he spent with Sylvie, but I can't account for the other five.

And he's probably thinking neither thing—

"Did you come with someone?" he asks, interrupting my mental digressions.

"No, you?"

"No." He shrugs in that I'm-so-hot-and-I-don't-even-know-it casual way of his that makes my knees go weak. "I'm working tonight. I designed the mosaic."

Work thing. He's alone. He must definitely be single.

"I know," I say.

"You do?"

"Yeah, I snatched up an invite to this party sort of hoping we could talk..." His forehead creases with curiosity and surprise, and before I can lose my nerve, I add, "Is there somewhere more private we can go talk?"

"Sure, follow me."

From the direction he takes, I know he's guiding me toward the hotel spa. In our previous visit, he showed me every ambient where one of his designs was up.

A server passes next to us, and Sam grabs two flutes of champagne from his tray.

He offers me one. "Does this conversation require wine?"

I take a glass. "Definitely."

After a quick sip, Sam shows me into the spa welcoming area. I remember it as an underwater castle with mermaids everywhere. But in this world, the walls portray a pond with a waterfall and two leopards drinking from the small lake.

"This is beautiful," I say, staring around. "I've always known you could make your dream come true, no matter what your parents said."

"Thank you." Sam stares at me expectantly, as if to say, *"But we're not here to discuss my job or my parents, are we?"*

An awkward silence stretches while I try to put my thoughts in a coherent order, but Sam surprises me by asking, "How have you been? I mean, I read about your company and saw the Forbes profile a few years back... it seems like you got everything you wanted, too..."

I look at him. "I have money, and I have a career, but it's not all I ever wanted..."

Another awkward silence follows. But this time, I take a deep breath and talk first. "Sam, what I'm about to say might sound strange, but please hear me out…"

"Okay," he says.

"A week ago, on Christmas Eve, I slipped on the ice and hit my head."

"Are you okay?"

"Yeah, yeah, I'm fine now, just a bump." Out of habit, I touch the spot at the back of my head. "But I spent Christmas night in a sort of medically induced coma." Sam's eyes goggle and I flutter my hands in a, "it's nothing serious," gesture. "And while I was in the coma, I had this weird dream, which felt more like I was sent to live in an alternative universe for a couple of months…"

Sam is staring at me with a skeptical but curious expression. "What was the dream about?"

I take a deep breath. "Well, in this other world, you and I had never split up. I'd stopped taking the pill that night you'd asked me and we'd gotten pregnant on the first try with our daughter Jo, Josephine. She is in the first grade now, and smart and pretty and so mature for her age. Will, our middle kid, likes to build bridges with books and he's such a picky eater, making him eat is torture, but he's also sweet and cuddly and still young enough that he lets us cover him with kisses whenever we want. And Bram, our youngest, he doesn't do much yet, but the other day he called me Mommy for the first time and it was the biggest emotion of my life. And you, you're an incredible dad. Present, and helpful. And we—we're a great team, really…"

Sam is staring at me, slightly slack-jawed. But now that I'm on a roll, I can't stop.

"And I'm not saying our life is all a bed of roses. I mean,

our house is a mess most of the time, and we live two doors down from my parents. Can you believe that? And I don't even mind because Mom is a great help with the kids. And our schedule is a nightmare and we have like three mortgages and three college funds to feed so we're not swimming in cash… and life gets complicated sometimes, like when we try to have sex and my breasts randomly leak milk because I'm still breastfeeding, or when the kids interrupt us, which happens most of the times…"

Sam grins. "Wow, you're really selling it hard to me now."

I laugh. "I know I sound completely crazy, but my dream felt so real…"

I stare behind his shoulder, expecting a mermaid and still finding two leopards.

Sam turns to look and then back at me. "You keep staring at the wall. Is something bothering you?"

"No, yes, sorry, it's just that in my dream this"—I gesture to the room—"was an ocean. The bamboo was a coral reef, the birds were fish and the leopards—"

"—a mermaid," we say in chorus.

Sam stares at me for a long moment. "How do you know that? I've drawn an alternative design, but I never showed it to anyone."

"I saw it in my dream. You'd chosen the ocean theme because Jo's favorite fairy tale is *The Little Mermaid* and she'd convinced you to go with water over jungle. We came here on New Year's Eve, we left the kids with a babysitter and spent the night in the magnolia suite."

Sam's eyebrows shoot high in his forehead. "That's the room they've given me." He looks astonished, like his head is spinning.

Next to the leopards, an indoor waterfall spurts out of the wall and ends in an artificial stream that runs for the length of the spa reception area. Sam now sits on the small stone wall that marks the riverbed and stares at me. "What are you saying that you saw an alternative future?"

I sit next to him. "I don't know if I traveled to a parallel dimension, or had a medication-induced hallucination, or a dream. But I want to make what I saw my reality, Sam, letting you go has been the biggest mistake of my life. All these years I thought I was doing great on my own until I saw how happy we could be together. We were *disgustingly* happy, Sam, like a Hallmark movie level happy…"

"That's vile," he says, mock disgusted. "Please don't tell me we hashtag our Instagram pics #blessed or I'm bailing right now."

I can't help but smile. "We don't, but we could."

Sam is joking along, but he's not saying much otherwise. I fidget with my dress and stare away. My gaze comes to rest on the rocks making up the riverbed where the fake waterfall lands. And a sudden inspiration hits me. I search the round, flat pebbles for a mostly dry one and grab a white one.

I don't have a pen, but I have lip gloss in my clutch. I use the pink brush to write yes on the stone.

Sam watches me, amused. "I don't think you're supposed to paint on hotel's properties."

I ignore the joke and look at him. "In my dream, you asked me if I wanted to try for another baby because you wanted another girl. And I said I wasn't sure because, you know, another pregnancy, and we'd have to clear the attic to make room for the baby and start another college fund. So, I said that I'd think about it. And you got super excited, but I told you to cool down because it wasn't a yes written in stone. But then my Christmas gift to you was a stone, engraved with a single word…"

"Yes?" Sam asks.

"Yes." I give him the pebble. "What I'm trying to say is that I want a second chance, I want to marry you, and go live in the suburbs, and have three, four, ten kids, as many as you want. And if we can't make them because you know we're sort of coming late to the race with my biological ticking clock and everything we can adopt, or I can freeze my eggs…" I trail off, finally out of words.

Sam is turning around the pebble in his hands.

"This would be a good moment to say something," I say. "I'm sort of dying over here."

Sam looks at me, deadly serious, every hint of a joke gone from his face. "When I broke up with you, I thought being a dad was the most important thing in my life. What I didn't realize was that wanting kids was only half of the equation… I also had to find a woman I wanted to have kids with, and after you, that never happened."

I chuckle nervously. "When I woke up from the coma, I waited an entire day before I had the guts to look you up on Facebook. I was dreading finding out you'd married young and already produced a football team of offspring."

"No." Sam's gaze stays intense. "You're the only woman I ever wanted to start a family with."

"If that's true, why didn't you reach out? You knew where I was."

"At first, it took me a few years to come to that conclusion… I might appear all mature and composed now, but I was a mess for a while after the breakup, more so because it had been my decision…"

"And later?"

"Well, the realization that there were women I could be in a relationship with, love even, but that I didn't want to marry or have kids with, convinced me I had been that kind of person for you… someone okay to date in college but not to start a family with…"

"Oh, Sam, no… back then, I prioritized the wrong things… you were right. We should've been young parents and not let work or money come between us. And it only took a coma and an otherworldly experience for me to realize what I had left behind… and in my dream, I realized that in all these years, I never stopped loving you. And I know this is *a lot* to take in that I'm sounding delirious, but we've wasted so much time, Sam, and I don't want to waste another minute. Not if I can help it."

"What are you proposing, Caroline? Marriage, a house in the suburbs, three to ten kids with relative college funds?" Sam stands up and offers me a hand. "Am I forgetting anything?"

I take his hand and let him pull me close. "An endless mess, and sleepless nights, and a few arguments along the way… and perhaps infrequent but very intense sex, and endless, disgusting happiness…"

"Endless, disgusting happiness… Yes, Charlie Bear." He flips the stone in the air once. "Yes. Written in stone."

With a cheeky smile, Sam throws the pebble back into the river and pulls me even closer, wrapping his arms around my lower back. His lips finally press onto mine just as the boom of fireworks explodes all over the city, signaling the beginning of a new year, of a new life…

Note from the Author

Dear Reader,

I hope you enjoyed A Christmas Caroline. This is the second book in the Christmas Romantic Comedy series, but it doesn't really matter if you started reading here or not, as all books in this series are complete standalones, totally unrelated to each other. Well, except that they share the same heartwarming, fuzzy holiday spirit. I hope you'll want to give the other books in the series a try as well.

The "next" book in the series will be Home for Christmas and it'll feature two families stuck in the same mountain cabin after a double-booking mishap.

Now, I have to ask you a favor. If you loved my story, **please leave a review** on Goodreads, your favorite retailer's website, or wherever you like to post reviews (your blog, your Facebook wall, your bedroom wall, in a text to your best friend...). Reviews are the best gift you can give to an author, and word of mouth is the most powerful means of book discovery.

Thank you for your constant support!

Camilla, x

PS. Did you notice my little Easter egg from A Sudden Crush? (Bucknam is the same publishing house Joanna Price was fired from in A Sudden Crush.)

Acknowledgments

Thank you to my son, Will and Bram characters are loosely based on him.

Many thanks to Silvia Meyer, a member of my Readers' Group, who suggested Sam's job. The idea of him being a mosaic designer tied in so beautifully with the story I'm still in awe.

Thank you to Rachel Gilbey for organizing the blog tour for this book and to all the book bloggers who participated. I love being part of your community.

Thank you to my street team, and to all of you who leave book reviews. They're so appreciated.

Thank you to all my readers. Without your constant support, I wouldn't keep pushing through the blank pages.

Thank you to my editors and proofreaders, Molly Hill at Both Barrels Author Services, Helen Baggott, and BBB Publishings for making my writing the best it could be.

And lastly, thank you to my family and friends for your constant encouragement.

Cover Image Credit: Created by Freepik

Made in the USA
Middletown, DE
16 December 2023